SPECIAL MESSAGE TO READERS

THE ULVERSCROFT FOUNDATION
(registered UK charity number 264873)

was established in 1972 to provide funds for research, diagnosis and treatment of eye diseases. Examples of major projects funded by the Ulverscroft Foundation are:-

- The Children's Eye Unit at Moorfields Eye Hospital, London
- The Ulverscroft Children's Eye Unit at Great Ormond Street Hospital for Sick Children
- Funding research into eye diseases and treatment at the Department of Ophthalmology, University of Leicester
- The Ulverscroft Vision Research Group, Institute of Child Health
- Twin operating theatres at the Western Ophthalmic Hospital, London
- The Chair of Ophthalmology at the Royal Australian College of Ophthalmologists

You can help further the work of the Foundation by making a donation or leaving a legacy. Every contribution is gratefully received. If you would like to help support the Foundation or require further information, please contact:

THE ULVERSCROFT FOUNDATION
The Green, Bradgate Road, Anstey
Leicester LE7 7FU, England
Tel: (0116) 236 4325

website: www.ulverscroft-foundation.org.uk

THE LION-TAMER'S DAUGHTER

When her family's circus is disbanded and her beloved lion Rexus moved to a private menagerie in Norfolk, Justine volunteers to spend a few weeks settling him in. Arriving at the stately home, she receives mixed reactions from the residents. Lady of the house Priscilla is aloof, while her two daughters seem just a little too curious about the lion. But groundsman Tom's welcome is warm, and as the two grow closer, can Justine keep everyone safe until it's time for her to leave and start a new life elsewhere?

Books by Henriette Gyland
in the Linford Romance Library:

BLUEPRINT FOR LOVE

HENRIETTE GYLAND

THE LION-TAMER'S DAUGHTER

Complete and Unabridged

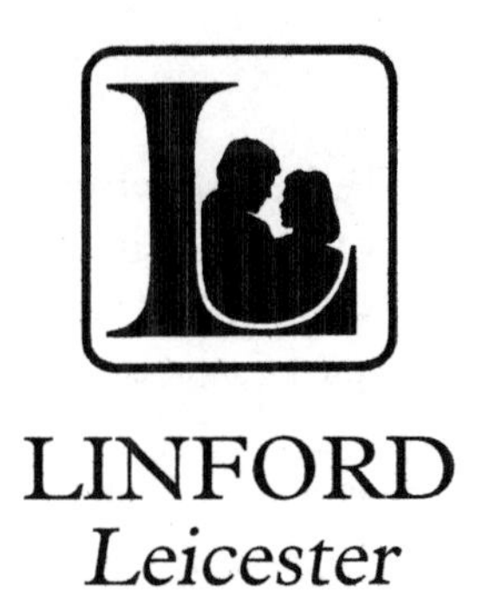

LINFORD
Leicester

First published in Great Britain in 2017

First Linford Edition
published 2020

A catalogue record for this book is available from the British Library.

ISBN 978–1–4448–4515–0

Published by
Ulverscroft Limited
Anstey, Leicestershire

Set by Words & Graphics Ltd.
Anstey, Leicestershire
Printed and bound in Great Britain by
T. J. International Ltd., Padstow, Cornwall

This book is printed on acid-free paper

1

Behind the curtain is where the circus begins and ends.

Justine's father Elijah spat in his palms for luck, then briefly clutched the crucifix around his neck and mouthed a silent prayer even though he wasn't particularly religious.

Around them performers were stretching, pacing, or taking giant gulps of air. Janos, Justine's eldest cousin, sat on the sawdust with his back against a pillar, his clown make-up smeared across his sweaty face after his exertions in the ring. Catching her eye, he sent her a tired grin.

She smiled back, then turned to watch the current performance through a gap in the curtain. Shrouded in shadows behind the heavy fabric, she held her breath as her aunt Yolande and her youngest cousin, Sara, reached the finale of their double trick-riding act. Her aunt by marriage came from a long line of Hungarian riders, said to be descendants of the Mongol hordes, and horsemanship was in her blood. Having recently been initiated into the craft, this was Sara's first whole season in the ring, and so far, no mishaps.

Justine crossed her fingers behind her back. Tonight was the last performance before the circus dispersed for the winter, and if Sara made a mistake now, it would be a bad omen.

The crowd wowed as both riders dropped to the ground on one side of the saddle, then back over the horse and the same on the other side before returning to the saddle again, where they rose and stretched their arms wide in perfect synchronicity with their horses.

The music changed to something more up-tempo to rouse the crowd as Yolande lowered herself over the side with her head down and her legs raised in the air. It was a move as graceful as it was daring, and although seemingly effortless, she held herself in place by the sheer strength in her arms.

Justine held her breath as Sara followed suit, slowly going over the side of her saddle, her blonde head perilously close to the horse's hooves.

One false move . . .

No, I won't think like that.

Sara had practised and practised, first using a harness, then without, but this was the first time the seventeen-year-old was riding upside down, a fitting finale to the current season.

The tension rose in beat with the music until both Sara and Yolande were in position. They did another turn of the ring, then when they were back in their saddles again with their arms held high, the music rose to a crescendo.

Success!

Sara had done it. Everyone had said she was too young, not physically strong enough, but circus kids went their own way, and Sara had insisted on copying her mother's act.

Beaming, she dropped from the

saddle next to her mother to receive the applause from the audience while the horses were led away by Justine's other cousin, Gabi, and a member of the ring crew. The performers followed shortly after, waving to the audience.

Janos quickly dabbed his face and grabbed a stuffed tiger toy.

'Go get 'em,' said Justine as he went past.

Janos sent her a clown grimace and bounced back into the ring, where preparations were already under way for the next act. As the ring crew began to erect the cage on the sawdust, Janos continued with his antics. Justine knew his act off by heart; he'd prance around the ring pretending to tame the tiger toy and getting it to perform. The toy would refuse to budge — obviously — and a seemingly exasperated Janos would perform the tricks the toy was supposed to do. The act would end with Janos somehow on the inside of the erected steel cage and the toy on the outside.

Kids would laugh, adults would point

to the toy and explain the significance, and everyone would know what was coming next — an act where audience perception of danger was greater than for all the others.

The big cats and their master.

Her father touched his crucifix again. Everyone had their own personal talisman or good luck charm. Justine's was a small square of cotton from a security blanket she'd had as a toddler, and which her ever-thoughtful mother, Beth, had cut off and saved for just such a purpose, before the rest of the blanket disintegrated.

It was small enough to fit in the palm of her hand, now sewn inside the bodice of her costume just above her heart. She placed her hand over it, took a deep breath, and went to stand beside her father.

'Ready?' he said in a low voice.

'As ready as I'll ever be,' she replied, her final ritual before a performance.

They entered the ring to the MC's introduction.

'La-adies and gen-tle-men! The one a-a-and only, the magnificent Belmont, and his beautiful assistant! Observe him tame the wi-i-ild beasts of the world!'

An exaggeration, but it worked. The crowd cheered and clapped as Justine and her father did their tour of the cage so the entire audience would get a glimpse of their faces set in grim determination against the forthcoming danger:

At least that was the idea.

Then, one by one, the animals were let into the ring through a tunnel cage.

'Behold the terrifying Rexus, straight from the African sa-a-avannah!' intoned the MC as the lion lumbered in and found his assigned pedestal to the far left, his home-away-from-home when out of his cage.

'Regard the fearsome tiger duo, Ajit and Mohan, the man-eaters of Ca-a-alcutta!'

Never mind that Rexus was bred in captivity and the young tiger twins came from a circus in Australia . . . The illusion was everything.

Ajit found his pedestal with no trouble, but Mohan snarled and clawed at Elijah's cane, his only defence against three large predators. There was a collective gasp from the audience, and a little girl at the front, who was here with her parents and grandfather by the looks of it, climbed onto her father's lap and promptly stuck her thumb in her mouth. The deep auburn hair of the little girl's father shone in the circus spotlight and caught Justine's attention. When her eyes met his — such dark, stormy blue eyes — through the bars of the cage, she nearly missed her footing and had to force her focus back on the animals.

Never turn your back on the tigers.

Elijah's first warning to Justine when she began assisting him rang out in her head. Male lions like Rexus were easier to tame because of their usually laidback nature, but tigers were more reserved and unpredictable.

She swallowed hard as her father

coaxed Mohan on to his pedestal, using soothing words, a titbit of meat, and the command 'Platz!' After what seemed like an age Mohan complied and sat on his pedestal with a smug grin on his face.

The audience cheered with relief, not knowing that it had been one such unruly tiger which had made Justine's mother Beth retire from the ring and take over catering instead. With a jagged scar on her arm to prove it.

When all three cats had settled, Elijah raised his cane and said, 'Up!' Rexus and the tigers sat up on their hind legs with their front paws in a begging pose and stayed on their hind legs for as long as Elijah held the cane in the air. When he lowered it again, the animals sat down.

A member of the ring passed three silver balls down the tunnel cage and Justine placed each of them in front of the animals.

'Seat!' Elijah raised and lowered his cane to command the tigers to climb onto the ball, and at the word 'Up!'

they raised themselves onto their hind legs, balancing on the balls. He then commanded Rexus onto his ball. The old lion did so but with a little less confidence, then when Elijah circled his finger in the air, the lion rolled the ball in a straight line to the edge of the cage grunting discontentedly, where he stopped, faltered a little when turning around, then back to his pedestal. 'Platz!' got him seated again.

The Irish audience responded with a roar of applause. They were every bit as appreciative as English audiences had been, more so perhaps. It made Justine's longing for her native country bearable as she still missed touring in England.

But there had been no other option for them than moving the circus to Ireland when the ban on performing with exotic animals in the UK came into effect. So far, it was still permitted here, and in many other parts of Europe too, but it probably wouldn't be long before those countries followed suit.

What her father would do then, Justine had no idea — he'd worked with big cats all his life, and his father and grandfather before him. She had her wire-walking act but Elijah had nothing else.

At her father's next signal Ajit and Mohan, still holding their position on the balls, did a tour of the ring and returned to their pedestals to rapturous applause from the audience. Mohan let out a short, sharp growl in response.

Elijah lowered his cane, commanded 'Home!' and the tigers jumped down from their pedestals and left the ring through the tunnel cage. Only Rexus was left.

Justine fetched three wooden blocks from a box at the back of the cage and placed them on the empty pedestal next to the lion.

The audience stilled. Rexus swished his plume-tipped tail as Elijah held two fingers up, then dropped his shaggy head to one side as if thinking deeply. After a moment's pause Rexus put his large paw on the wooden block with the number '2' and pushed it to the ground.

The audience cheered. Elijah held up three fingers, and this time Rexus pushed the number '3' block. When Elijah held up one finger on one hand and four fingers on the other, Rexus nudged number '5' from the pedestal. Predictably, the crowd erupted, and the roar of a lion pleased with himself filled the tent.

When the applause had finally died down, Justine sat on the pedestal in the middle, and at Elijah's subtle signal, there was a whoosh of air and the smell of musk as four hundred pounds of sinewy and muscular flesh leapt over her sequinned shoulder and landed on the pedestal on her other side.

Rising, she struck a ballet pose to present Rexus's manoeuvre as the crowd clapped enthusiastically, applause which morphed into a standing ovation when Elijah wrapped his arms around the lion and tousled his shaggy mane.

Cameras flashed, sequins twinkled, sawdust and the scent of the animals filled Justine's nostrils, Rexus's contented purring in her ears.

It was over.

2

3 months later

Snow crunched under Justine's UGG boots as she trampled across the snowy yard to the big top, which was how circus people referred to the big tent. Every year Circus Belmont overwintered in Suffolk, renting land and premises from the same farmer, although this year they were in the neighbouring county of Norfolk. Grumpily she stuck out her tongue to catch a snowflake, but mainly because she felt like sticking her tongue out at the world.

This was the third strategy meeting in as many weeks, an unusual occurrence in the winter months when her family and the core staff would hunker down to work on new acts for the next season, repair costumes and equipment, and tend to the animals.

There was no denying it; the circus was in trouble, and this time for real.

Justine stopped and squinted up at the tent in the wintry half-light. Normally it was festooned with gaudy banners proclaiming the talents of the performers as well as bunting flapping enticingly in the breeze, but this evening the thick yellow vinyl covering, cold and wet with falling snow, looked almost grey. Inside it would be no warmer except for the ring — why waste heating on punters who weren't there?

She lifted the heavy tarpaulin that functioned as a door and shook the snow off her boots on the fake grass doormat.

Elijah stood in the centre of the ring addressing everyone who had arrived before Justine. Always the showman, even in overalls, he paused for dramatic effect as she entered, and glared at her.

'About bloody time,' he grumbled.

'Sorry, I was talking to Rexus,' she replied as she high-fived Janos, then plonked herself down on the woodchip-strewn floor next to Sara who glistened with sweat from training and smelled of horse. Despite her obvious exertions Sara sat huddled in a fleece and had chosen a spot next to a Calor gas heater. Justine unzipped her jacket.

'Rexus doesn't talk,' said her father.

'Oh, he does, and the things he tells me . . . '

'Enough of your cheek, young lady.' Elijah turned to his brother. 'Jethro, I'll let you take it from here.'

Justine's throat went dry, and she noticed Sara swallowing hard. In addition to working as MC and artistic director, Uncle Jethro was also in charge of the circus finances. A hush fell as if they all knew what was coming next.

'I'm not one for pussyfooting around the issue,' he said, voice booming out of habit rather than fear they couldn't hear him, 'so I'll go straight to the point. We're closing the doors on Circus Belmont. We simply can't afford to keep going any longer.'

The ring erupted with anger and disappointment, and it was some time before anyone could make themselves heard.

'Where will everyone go?' asked Janos, raising his voice.

Gabi cleared his throat. 'There's no work out there unless you want to clean streets.'

'Is there nothing you can do? You can halve my pay if you like,' shouted the head of the ring crew.

Jethro answered each question with his usual self-assurance as they were fired at him, repeating the fact that nothing would help, but no one seemed to be listening. The circus had been going for generations of the Belmont family, nearly a hundred and fifty years by Justine's reckoning, and the loss of livelihood wasn't people's only concern. There was tradition and pride, a sense of belonging too. Things you couldn't measure in dry figures.

Jethro remained patient. He'd always

been kind and supportive of the children, carrying on in the same manner even as they all grew up, whereas for Justine's own father and her aunt Yolande it was always hard graft and no moaning.

Practice does not make perfect. Only perfect practice makes perfect. Practice, practice, practice. She knew the mantra in her dreams. It made sense, of course, but still it annoyed her to have it shoved down her throat from dawn to dusk.

She longed to ask her uncle what was truly going on, if this really was the end, as she doubted her father would tell her anything, but Jethro's face gave nothing away. She sighed. He probably couldn't tell her anything that Elijah hadn't shared already.

This time, however, her father surprised her. When everyone had calmed down a little, Elijah took centre stage again.

'We cannot compete with the Russians and the Chinese, or even Cirque du Soleil despite their higher ticket fees. We have a toothless old lion — '

'Rexus isn't toothless,' Justine protested, crossing her arms. She still bore the puncture marks on her shin from the time a snotty-nosed brat had sneaked onto the back lot between the tents and the caravans and provoked the lion while she was feeding him in his cage. 'And he isn't old.'

' — a few horses, trapezes, a line dancer — ' only then did Elijah glance at Justine despite her rude interruption ' — a clown — ' he lifted an eyebrow at Janos.

'Plus the dog trainers, who come back every year,' he continued. 'I know the spaniels attract families with young children but it's not enough. We have other travelling acts too, but truth be told, we're old hat. People want something different, something that can awe them more than special effects, and they're already spoiled for choice, what with films and computer games.'

'Don't the tigers attract people?' asked Gabi.

'We won't survive another season.

That's what Jethro has been trying to tell you. The spaniels saw an upswing in audience numbers but it dropped again after a while. The same happened with the tigers even without Rexus, and perhaps they might hold the interest for longer, perhaps not. I'm not prepared to gamble on the next season when we're already in the red. Anyway, Beth and I are ready to move onto something different.'

Justine turned to her mother who until now had been sitting quietly at the edge of the ring. 'Like what?'

'Catering,' said Beth simply. 'Your father feels he's getting too old to handle big cats, and together we've been offered a job to be in charge of catering for a German circus when the next season starts. That way he can still be around lions.'

'And when were you planning on telling me?' Justine muttered.

'It's about ending on an up-note,' Beth added, her soft brown eyes darkening at the memory of her injury, which had been severe enough to scare even the most hardened circus performers.

Elijah grimaced. 'What your mum is trying to say is that I'm not the man I used to be. Jethro and Yolande are in agreement that we must close, not just because the cats are too much for me.'

'And what's going to happen to all the animals? And the equipment?' asked Justine.

'I've been trying to figure that out. The horses will go to a riding school. They're well-mannered and docile enough for children to ride them. Gabi has been offered a job there if he'll take it, and Janos, as we all know, is going to agricultural college next September.'

'I'll take it,' said Gabi. 'Better than cleaning streets anyhow.'

Justine experienced a sudden lump in her throat. She'd known all three horses from foal, and she often helped Sara and Yolande train with them when she wasn't practising her act on the line or working with her father. Then an even worse feeling stole over her.

'What about the rest of the animals? Rexus and the boys?'

Her father sent her a long look, and she held her breath while she waited for him to say something she couldn't bear to hear, that none of them could bear to hear, least of all Elijah himself who'd had the lion for many years. A zoo would probably take the tigers but who would have any use for a fifteen-year-old lion?

'No,' she said before he spoke. 'You can't do it! I won't let you!' She jumped up as Sara started sobbing quietly.

Elijah sighed. 'You misunderstand me. He won't be put down. He'll retire. A private menagerie has promised to take him. It's based in Norfolk, near the coast so not too far from here, and run by an eccentric old man. Rexus will be able to live out his days in comfort if not excitement.'

'So you're just giving him away?'

'I can't bring him with me to my new job. Surely you can see that?'

Justine frowned. She'd heard her

father talk about retiring from the ring for a number of years now but she'd never really believed him. It had seemed half-hearted somehow, a romantic dream perhaps, but now she realised he'd been serious all along. Not only that, she wondered how well she knew him, knew either of her parents, when it came to it.

Sara was still sobbing, and Gabi and Janos sat with their heads bowed. This was all the four cousins had ever known. They had grown up in this extended family unit, each with their own role to fulfil, a unit which had exploded to three times their numbers during the travelling season, creating excitement and variation. If it had sometimes felt as if work was relentless and never-ending, it had brought its own rewards.

And now they were disbanded. Just like that.

Angry tears pressed behind her eyes. 'But he will miss us,' she said, even as she knew her father was making perfect sense.

'I know, and we'll miss him. That's

why I've arranged it so that you go with him and see him settled in. The owners have agreed for you to stay a few weeks, or for as long as it takes. And after that . . . ' Her father smiled for the first time since she'd entered the tent, a soft warm smile which changed his demeanour completely, making him the father she knew and loved.

'You're twenty-three, my love. It's time you followed your own path. Maybe joined another circus where you can further your career. Or maybe something else will come along, who knows.'

This was more than Justine could bear. She snatched up her jacket and stormed out of the performance tent. Outside she turned her face towards the sky, letting the snowflakes cool her angry flush.

The trouble was, her father was right. If the circus was to close, it made sense for her to sign up with another outfit, but she realised now that she'd never been apart from her family for more than a few days at a time.

Was she truly ready for that?

* * *

'You did *what*?'

Cousin Henry folded his *Financial Times* and placed it beside the remnants of his breakfast. The delicate bone china teacup rattled in the saucer as he laid the newspaper down more forcefully than he'd probably intended.

Not one for losing his cool, at thirty-two he looked much like he had ten years ago: conservative haircut, well-manicured hands, primly dressed in shirt and chinos. The perfect country gentleman who wouldn't look out of place at a polo match.

Only a deep frown gave away his concerns; his wife was expensive and his daughters spoiled little tearaways.

Well, they were lovely really, but sometimes Tom was tempted to read his cousin's children the Riot Act.

'I thought we'd agreed not to indulge

the old man's crazy ideas,' said Henry. 'And you've bought a lion. I give up, I really do!'

Tom ran his fingers through his unruly mop of auburn hair, a feature he'd inherited from his mother and cursed many times over. He normally tied it back with an elastic band, but today he'd left it loose on a whim. But whatever he did with it, he could never be as polished as Henry.

'I didn't buy it, exactly. A retiring circus owner gave it to us for free.'

'Well, that's something, I suppose,' Henry replied, 'although it'll probably eat us out of house and home. What *do* lions eat, come to think of it?'

'Meat. Lots of it.' Tom grinned. 'On a more serious note — '

'As if this isn't serious enough,' Henry muttered.

'I caught Dilly pulling the cat's tail again, quite hard this time.'

Henry shrugged. 'Oh, she's just high-spirited. They both are. She'll grow out of it.'

Another word entirely sprang to Tom's mind, but he kept it to himself. Instead he said, 'Henry, she's six. She's not a toddler and should know better. It's high time they both learned that animals have feelings, and what better teacher than an animal which can induce some respect at the same time?'

'I'm not having my daughters anywhere near that beast!'

'Of course not, I'm just saying it's a way to learn about animals. They'll be home for the Christmas holidays soon anyway.'

'Talking of Christmas, Priscilla wants to invite half the country. How can I afford what she calls 'necessary expenses for a man in my position'?' Groaning, Henry rubbed his hands over his face. 'She acts as though I'm lord of the manor, which I'm not and may never be — as well she knows.'

Contrary to what most people assumed, Henry wasn't the heir to Stonybrook. He would inherit the title of baronet when his grandfather, the current baronet, died, but because the estate wasn't entailed upon the eldest son of the family, it would only come to him if his grandfather left it to him. As steward he was given a salary by the estate, which he was happy with but his wife wasn't, with his wife's lifestyle founded on the expectation that the estate would go to her husband eventually. Tom thought it a lost cause — Lord Brooks had never got over losing both his sons before their time, and it had made him a little eccentric. He still maintained that he could, and would, will it to whomever he wanted.

Henry had accepted the situation and that his hands were tied financially, and Tom did what he could to help, drawing only a small salary from his work on the estate grounds. He'd also come up with a few money-making ideas in the last couple of years, such as leasing the last of the arable land to a neighbouring farmer, opening the gardens to the public, applying for grants, and refurbishing the Victorian private menagerie which the old man insisted on keeping, but which could be turned into a small private zoo one day. That was the plan anyway.

Tom considered himself blessed that both his own parents were alive and well; life had not been quite so easy for Henry. Perhaps that explained why he was always so anxious.

'You needn't worry about the lion. The circus owner is sending a trainer to stay for a few weeks to see the animal settled. Personally I don't think that's necessary. I worked with big cats for that reservation in Africa, and would prefer to do it myself. That would be one less responsibility for you.'

Henry shook his head as if to himself. 'With my wife's extravagant Christmas plans and a carnivore to feed it hardly matters. But you need to check with Priscilla where she wants to put the trainer up. I expect some of our guests will be staying after the Christmas party.'

'Check what with Priscilla?'

Just then Henry's wife appeared, immaculate as ever in designer jeans and high heels, her blonde hair artfully arranged in a bun, which was both ordered and deliberately messy at the same time. Sexy too.

Tom looked away, aware that Priscilla knew the effect she had on men. He'd sworn to stay away from women like that, women who knew their own worth — which in itself wasn't a bad thing — and who knew how to exploit it. Which *was* a bad thing.

His thoughts turned briefly to his ex-wife Jennifer who'd bulldozed into his life expecting great things from his connections with a baronet, only to bulldoze out again when she realised those connections came with no financial advantage. She had taken him to the cleaners, and he'd let her because winning meant everything to her and nothing to him. The sooner he saw the back of her, the better.

Thank God they'd had no children to fight over.

Which was why he was now living here with his cousin's family at Stonybrook — which he privately referred to as Stonybroke — working as groundsman and gamekeeper, a role he filled well enough even if it took him far away from his dreams of Africa. A lion in the grounds was the next best thing.

'What am I required to do?' Priscilla repeated, intruding into Tom's thoughts.

'There's a lion arriving any time now and it comes with a trainer who'll need accommodation for a while.'

'A lion? You *are* kidding me, right?'

'He's not,' said Henry, with a sigh. 'Apparently Grandfather has acquired an old lion from a circus to live in the enclosure, and a trainer of sorts is coming to stay for a while. He's had cats before, but — '

'Before we met, yes.' A muscle worked in Priscilla's jaw, and her eyes bored into Tom's. Then she shrugged. 'He can stay in the flat above the garages,' she said, clearly more concerned with hospitality arrangements than the arrival of a lion. 'That way he can take his animal smells direct to his own bathroom without going through the house. He's no doubt an outdoorsy type so probably won't have a problem lighting the wood burner. And there are electric heaters too,' she added, to show her generosity.

'That'll be fine. I'm sure he isn't used to any kind of luxury.'

'No, I should imagine not,' said Priscilla in a neutral tone but with just enough disdain to indicate it was with great forbearance only that she tolerated the riff-raff the baronet forced them to mingle with, and that Tom would back him up.

'As I said to Henry, I'd be happy to deal with the animal myself, so it may not even be relevant,' Tom added.

'Well, good. The sooner he's gone, the better.'

3

The lion arrived in the early morning on a rainy day. It was still dark, and a slight mist hung in the air, which even the bright fairy lights covering the topiary laurel bush in the centre of the drive couldn't chase away. Tom stood on the steps next to Lord Brooks who had insisted, in his usual cantankerous manner, that he wanted to be there to welcome the beast, despite the chill of the morning.

'Stop mollycoddling me!' Richard grumbled when Tom had tried to persuade him to stay indoors in the warmth.

Tom shrugged. There was no point in arguing with Richard once he got an idea in his head. Instead he made sure the old man wore a thick overcoat and waited far enough back to be sheltered by the portico.

Smiling to himself, Tom smelled the freshness of the air as the raindrops bounced upwards and caressed his face like microscopic butterflies.

A day of promise.

The driver had called ten minutes previously and asked for directions from the main road, and now the large transit van pulled up on the circular gravelled forecourt leaving deep tyre impressions in the neatly raked gravel.

Tom grinned as he imagined Priscilla's face; she wouldn't be happy about that. Not that she'd done any of the raking herself.

Three people jumped out of the cab, energetically and seemingly unfazed by the wet weather. Elijah Belmont and his wife Beth, whom Tom had already met, and a young man whom he took to be a relative of Elijah's judging by the vague family resemblance. Then the back of the van opened, and a girl climbed out.

Young woman, he corrected himself. Very much a woman. He recognised her as the lion tamer's assistant when he went to Ireland in the summer with Richard and Henry's family, and he, Priscilla and the old man had taken the girls to the circus while Henry conducted some business. He remembered how he'd caught her eyes, and she appeared to miss a step. Back then he'd imagined it was because he'd had some sort of effect on her, but that was probably his mind playing tricks on him.

A warm feeling stole over him. Without all her circus glitter and heavy makeup she appeared younger somehow, vulnerable even. Which was probably his imagination as well.

He swallowed hard, refusing to allow his head to be turned, and stepped forward to shake Elijah's hand, then his wife's. Mrs Belmont had an unusually firm grip for a woman, or at least like the kind of woman Tom usually met.

'Welcome to Stonybrook,' he said. 'I'm Tom Yates. I work on the grounds here.'

The young man stepped forward to

shake his hand as well.

'My nephew, Gabi,' Elijah explained. 'And this is my daughter, Justine.'

Tom moved to greet her but she kept her hands in her pockets of her hoodie and stared at him with undisguised hostility. He dropped his hand but kept a cooler smile in place and tried to make a joke of her rudeness.

'What did I do?'

'Rexus belongs with us,' she replied without preamble.

'Ah, well . . . ' Elijah shrugged. 'You must forgive my daughter. I'm afraid that not everyone in our family is in agreement with my plans for the animals.'

'It happens, in families,' said Tom but kept his eyes on the girl, struck by how different she looked to her parents: blonde with wide green eyes in contrast to her father's still black hair — dyed? — and dark almond-shaped eyes. Mrs Belmont was dark too.

'And this is . . . ' Tom turned to indicate Richard on the steps, but he had disappeared. 'Oh, er, I was going to introduce you to Lord Brooks, but he must've gone back inside.'

'Ah well, it's a chilly morning.' Elijah Belmont rubbed his hands against the cold. 'Can't say I blame him. I'm sure we'll meet another time. Let's get Rexus settled, then,' he added. Was it Tom's imagination, or did the circus owner sound relieved?

He didn't have time to ponder Richard's sudden disappearance when, with the agility Tom had always associated with circus folk, the young woman swung up on the back step of the van and opened the doors further to reveal a metal animal transfer cage.

'Hold on, cuz.' Speaking for the first time, Elijah's nephew put a hand on hers. 'We need to know where they want him, and then get the van as close as possible. He's a heavy old bastard, after all.'

The cousins exchanged a look, the kind that comes from knowing each other very well, but with tenderness too, Tom thought, and a peculiar pang hit him in the chest which he only vaguely recognised as a sudden, raging jealousy. Of course they were bound to be close — working and living together as circus people did would surely create a special bond but it left him with a feeling of being very much on the outside and looking in on someone else's togetherness.

The girl stopped what she was doing and nodded briefly, her mouth set in a firm line and eyes shiny. Tears? Surely not; she seemed far too tough for that.

And yet . . . when her eyes caught his, he saw that he'd been right.

'He . . . Rexus, isn't it?' She nodded. 'He'll be all right here,' he said.

She nodded again, less grimly this time, and with the faintest trace of a smile. Tom suddenly wanted to reach out and pull her into a hug but realised she'd likely bite his head off.

But it was a good beginning.

Beginning? *What are you like?* There would be no beginning with any woman for a long time, not even green-eyed goddesses like this prickly circus girl.

★ ★ ★

I remember you.

Not many men had red hair like that and wore it so unashamedly loose like a rose gold crown. This groundsman — Tom — was the reason Justine had nearly missed a step during the last performance of the season. As far as she was aware ginger men preferred to keep their hair cropped short or even shaved off, fearing that it would make them look effeminate. Or something like that.

There was nothing effeminate about this guy. On the contrary, Justine thought, drinking in his broad shoulders, strong hands and sturdy workman's clothes. He was every bit a man.

Heat rose in her face. She tore her gaze away and jumped back in the cab next to her parents, while Gabi rode in the groundsman's Jeep to the far end of the park surrounding the estate.

Here her concerns eased when she saw the enclosure where Rexus would live out the rest of his days. A chain-link perimeter fence was built around the standard two-and-five-eighths inch steel posts no more than ten feet apart, sunk in concrete and reaching as high as sixteen feet with no roof. A so-called 'tiger trail'.

There were two smaller cages adjoining it, one housing a pair of drowsy hyenas, the second appearing to be empty until a curious porcupine, woken from its sleep, waddled into view. Further away was a dilapidated aviary, but no birds. A spectator barrier consisting of a series of wooden posts and wooden planks, one chest-high and one lower down, ran along the front and sides of the three cages. Lithe as a panther Gabi slipped between the planks and tested the strength of the fence, which didn't move an inch when he yanked at it.

'This looks fairly new,' he commented.

'It's about ten years old,' Tom explained. 'Lord Brooks has had large cats before so it's always been well-maintained. The only thing I've changed is the inward sloping fencing on the top. Originally we thought of building an exterior perimeter fence around the enclosure as extra security, but the only animals we've had here have been quite old and too lazy to bother to escape.'

Justine could see why the old lion might not consider escaping. In the centre of the enclosure a line of stone boulders were placed around a stone-lined pool, which together with the sheer size of it — about 600 square feet at a guess — created a perfect exercise area. To the side two indoor cages gave the animal access from the enclosure, and the animal carer could enter a separate area from outside, to feed the animals and clear out the cages while empty.

'It's . . . perfect,' she said and wished she could forget her resentment that this rich old man — whom she'd only glimpsed briefly when she jumped out of the back of the van — could afford to keep Rexus when the circus couldn't.

And that this red-haired scruff would be looking after him, and she would have to leave him.

Shoving her hands in her pockets, she watched as Gabi and her father unloaded Rexus's transport cage and pushed it towards the habitat gate at the back of the enclosure, while her mother stayed in the van to complete the paperwork. Gabi then slid the cage door open for Rexus to enter the enclosure, but the lion refused to budge.

'Nngh,' he grunted as Elijah prodded him with the end of his cane.

'Come on, my old friend,' her father said. 'This is your new home. Bigger than anything you've ever had.'

'Nngh,' the lion grunted again and swiped half-heartedly at the cane.

'Justine?' Elijah said.

'Sure.'

* * *

Tom watched as the girl disappeared into the back of the van and returned with a bucket with a tightly closed lid.

Bribery, he thought, as she let the lion sniff a large slab of raw meat through the bars of the transport cage before throwing it inside the enclosure.

The lion looked at her with large — and sad? — eyes, then grunted again before turning his back on the enclosure and the food.

'This isn't working,' said Elijah. 'I'll have to get in there.'

'Let me do it,' said the girl.

'What?' Tom looked from father to daughter, then fixed his eyes on the girl. 'You're not serious.'

She shrugged. 'Rexus won't budge otherwise, if he's in a mood.'

With mounting horror Tom watched as Elijah and the nephew closed the transport cage again, backed it up a little for Elijah's daughter to slip in through the gap and inside the enclosure with the bucket of meat.

'Are you absolutely out of your

mind? It's a frigging lion!'

The girl sent him a scathing look through the fence. 'Yes, I know. *My* lion.'

'Don't do it!' he shouted as the nephew slid open the cage door. He grabbed hold of the fence, ready to launch himself over the top and pull this crazy girl to safety.

Smiling properly for the first time, she approached the fence and touched his fingers through the wire mesh. 'It'll be fine. I'll be fine. I know Rexus very well, I can read his moods like an open book. Best if you step back a little, I think he senses your fear.'

'But — '

'Just back away,' she ordered, and Tom found himself backing away from the fence, his feet reacting before his mind, such was her quiet confidence.

The girl pulled a slab of meat out of the bucket, and the old lion left the transport cage to take the titbit offered to him. Then she emptied the remaining meat into a trough and stepped out of the enclosure while the lion was preoccupied.

Turning to Tom, she sent him a dazzling smile, which made his heart skip a beat.

'See? Easy-peasy. No need for you to worry.'

'If you say so,' he mumbled, still trying to compose himself after her smile and her fearless act.

'I do say so.'

* * *

'Justine will stay here for a few weeks, just until Rexus is settled,' said Elijah as the five of them were eating brunch in the estate kitchen some time later. The snooty lord hadn't reappeared, but circus folk were used to people being suspicious of them, sometimes even looking down on them, and Justine saw no reason to dwell on it.

It was a large, comfortable room with a scrubbed pine table at one end and a shiny range cooker at the other. Copper pots and pans hung from the ceiling above the cooker, more for show she thought as they were absolutely massive, and the kitchen units themselves had been painted cream, with a few scuffs in the paintwork here and there which added to the homely feel. Pots of herbs dotted the windowsills, and clean crockery was drying on a wooden dish drainer.

The kitchen had been decorated for Christmas, with a tasteful garland of holly — fake but a convincing fake — tacked on to the bottom edge of the wall cabinets, and on a tall dresser against the back wall stood an oval silver dish filled with gold baubles so shiny Justine could see her own reflection in each of them.

'I beg your pardon?'

Shock registered on the groundsman's face before he managed to disguise it.

'The girl? That won't be necessary.'

'Yes, the *girl*,' she snapped. 'As you saw, I know Rexus well. I want to see him settled properly, and I'll be damned if I'm going to let some jumped-up gamekeeper tell me what to do, even if you are the new owner.' She stuck out her chin in defiance.

'And I'll be damned if I'm going to let some slip of a girl get in the way of my work. I've worked with large cats before, here as well as in Africa and — '

'Slip of a girl? Well, I bet I worked with large animals before you were out of nappies!'

'Oh, yeah? Well, I know this estate like the back of my hand, and I don't need any interfe — '

Elijah held up his hands. 'Whoa, no need for this kind of talk.'

'Met your match, cuz?' Gabi sniggered.

Justine sent him a dirty look, which just made him laugh even harder.

'As I said, it won't be necessary,' the groundsman repeated.

Elijah shook his head. 'All the same, I would appreciate it if you'd extend this courtesy to my daughter. It would mean a lot to her.'

Justine met the groundsman's eyes, and as he stared back, she noticed a softening in his expression at her father's words. A curious, tingly feeling stole down her spine and pooled in her belly. Suddenly this wasn't all about Rexus anymore.

He held her eyes a little longer before nodding. 'All right. I suppose I could do with a little help with the animal.'

Her father and the groundsman continued discussing what she'd be doing and the practicalities surrounding her stay at the estate, almost as if she wasn't there, but it didn't matter. Her mother winked at her. She'd won.

For the time being.

* * *

Elijah, his wife and nephew left around midday. Tom watched Mrs Belmont pulling her daughter into what appeared to be a slightly awkward embrace, judging by their rigid postures.

'I'm all right, Mum,' the girl protested.

'I know, it's just . . . Stay safe, baby.' Mrs Belmont swiped a hand across her eyes.

How odd, Tom thought. It wasn't like they were saying goodbye forever.

Gabi tossed a holdall at his cousin in an offhand manner, which took Tom by surprise, but Justine caught it with apparent ease, reminding Tom of the strength behind her elfin looks.

'So, where do I sleep?' she asked as the van carrying her family disappeared down the winding lane to the manor house.

'Eh . . . ' Tom ran his fingers through his hair. Priscilla had said something about accommodation, but he couldn't for the life of him remember what. There was something about this girl that made him forget half of himself. 'My cousin's wife Priscilla deals with that side of things. She runs the household, while Henry manages the estate. Come, let me introduce you.

They should be back from their outing by now.'

He moved to take her bag, but she kicked it out of his reach.

'I'll be fine.'

'I insist.'

Their eyes clashed, for the second time, but this time he held her stare. In the end she sighed and pushed the bag towards him with her foot.

'It's your funeral.'

He grimaced as he lifted up the bag, which was as heavy as he'd expected it to be. 'At this rate, that might be quite soon.'

She laughed. 'I tried to pack as little as possible, but, well . . . I'm a woman.'

'No doubt about that.'

Tom led the way to the small drawing room where Henry and Priscilla were likely to be at this hour, leading Justine through the kitchen where they'd had brunch, because he suspected she would prefer that to going through the grandiose hall with its portraits of forbidding-looking ancestors. At any rate, he preferred entering through the kitchen himself.

* * *

A picture of classy domesticity presented itself to Justine when Tom opened the door to what must be the main drawing room.

There were more Christmas decorations here. Another emerald green garland with elaborately tied magenta bows, decorative poinsettias, golden tassels and trailing, glittered tendrils adorned the mantelpiece, and a real Christmas tree in the corner of the room reached almost to the ceiling and twinkled with silver baubles, silver lametta and white ribbons. An angel with white silken wings surveyed it all from the top of the tree. The scent of pine filled the room.

Justine couldn't help it. Her mouth fell slightly open at the excess.

The lord and lady — or whatever they were; Justine had no real idea about these people — and two young girls sat around a spindly-legged coffee table, each engaged in their own pursuits. The man was reading the paper, the woman a glossy magazine, while the two girls, one of them with her legs dangling over the armrest of a Regency-style chair, stared intently at their iPads. A white Persian cat lay curled up on a footstool under the coffee table.

All of them, apart from the man, were dressed in jeans, and with the modern coffee cups on the table, they seemed strangely out of place in this old-fashioned, high-ceilinged room with its mullioned windows overlooking the park.

'Henry, Priscilla, this is Justine who'll be looking after the lion with me,' said Tom.

The youngest of the two girls jumped up from her chair. 'Has it arrived? Can we go see it?'

She had blue eyes, wide with wonder, and her straight brown hair looked as if she'd attempted to brush it but with little success. She reminded Justine of a younger version of her cousin Sara, and she had to resist the temptation to reach out and pull the little girl into a big hug.

'Dilly,' her mother admonished as she closed her magazine and placed it neatly on the table with a perfectly manicured hand.

'I'll take you later,' Tom replied.

The man — Henry, fair hair, pleasant face — got up and came towards Justine with a beaming smile and shook her hand warmly.

'Apologies, we've been out for the morning. I hope Tom has been looking after you,' he said.

'Thank you, we had lunch in your lovely kitchen.'

'Good, good. Anyway, you must be the famous lion-tamer. Welcome to Stonybrook. I'm Henry, the steward. This is my wife Priscilla — ' he indicated the glamorous woman who nodded curtly ' — and my daughters

Portia and Cordelia, but we call her Dilly. Please make yourself welcome and feel free to stay as long as you wish.'

'I appreciate it. But it's actually my father who's the lion-tamer. I'm only his assistant.'

'Only an assistant?' Priscilla rose slowly and held out a limp-wristed hand for Justine to shake. 'Will you be able to manage the lion, then?'

'I know Rexus very well. I'll manage just fine.'

Perhaps Priscilla's concern was meant kindly, but her words irritated Justine. She met Priscilla's cool blue eyes square on and was surprised to see them widen, almost as if they'd met before. Which they had, in a way, as she'd been the woman sitting next to Tom during Circus Belmont's last performance, the one Justine had thought was Tom's wife.

'And do you have no role of your own in your, uhm, circus?'

'I do. I'm a wire-walker.'

'I beg your pardon?'

'A line-dancer,' Justine explained.

'A line-dancer?' The older of the girls spoke for the first time. 'Sick!'

'Portia!' Priscilla arched her eyebrows.

'I mean, that's very . . . interesting,' the girl added. Icy blonde like her mother, she schooled her features into an inscrutable expression, but Justine caught a mischievous gleam in her clever eyes.

Justine smiled. '*I* like it. Perhaps I can teach you sometime.'

'Me too! Me too!' shouted Cordelia.

'I don't think so, girls.' Priscilla clapped her hands. 'Now, haven't you got any homework you should be doing?'

'It's the school holidays, Mummy,' replied Portia with a slight roll of her eyes.

'Then you can spend some time practising the piano. And you, Dilly, the violin. Now, off you go. I need to organise sleeping arrangements for Miss . . . ?'

'Belmont,' Justine replied. 'Marie Justine Belmont. But you can call me Justine.'

'Very well. Let me show you to your

rooms. Henry, please take the girls for their music practice. Tom, I'll take over from here.'

'Okeydokey.' He winked at Justine as Priscilla narrowed her eyes at him.

Priscilla practically ushered Justine out of the drawing room as if her mere presence was polluting the air. Justine smiled to herself; this wasn't the first time she'd been treated as a cross between a gypsy and the paid entertainment, and she'd developed a thick skin against it.

'I'll show you the rest of the estate tomorrow,' Tom called after her as Priscilla closed the door behind them.

'This way,' said Priscilla. 'If you like, I can get Tom to take your bag up later.'

'Thank you, but I'm all right.'

Priscilla glanced at the bag, then back at Justine, and shrugged. Justine followed her, not up the stairs as she'd expected, but out through the kitchen again, across the cobbled yard at the back, which Justine had noticed earlier was flanked by outbuildings on three sides, and up an outdoor, winding staircase at the gable of one of the outbuildings.

'The garages are down below,' Priscilla explained. 'This used to be the chauffeur's flat, but we don't have a chauffeur any longer,' she added with a sigh.

'Right.'

'It's quite comfortable if a little outdated. There's no central heating, but I figured that wouldn't be a problem for you since you must be used to living jn a caravan.'

'It won't be a problem.' Although she was used to comments like that, delivered in a certain tone, hairs prickled on the back of Justine's neck. That it was designed to make her feel inferior was confirmed by Priscilla's next words.

'You won't be in anyone's way here, and can go about your business with the . . . animal as you please.'

'Sure.'

Having unlocked the door, Priscilla handed Justine the key and yanked open the curtains covering a large French balcony overlooking the cobbled yard, and revealed a sitting room with a small kitchen, and with another door at the far end of the room.

The bedroom, Justine assumed, and hoped it had a bathroom so she didn't have to steal across to the house to have a wash. To her relief she was right, and it even featured a large, claw-footed bathtub, a luxury she'd never experienced before.

Priscilla opened the curtains in the bedroom to another French balcony and pointed across the yard. 'Because the grounds are open to the public we have a small tearoom over there, in what used to be the old stables. Tom's idea.'

She sighed again. Clearly not her idea.

Looking across at the red brick building, Justine noticed flowerpots and ornaments behind the windows of the stables. A shop sign with the single word 'café' hung above the double doors, and a blackboard outside proclaimed today's specials, but Justine was too far away to make out what these were. An old-fashioned, stone mounting-block in the corner of the yard outside the café was the only evidence that this building was once the stables. The sight of the mounting block made her frown — so tempting for a young child to clamber on and fall down onto the cobbles.

Memories of the countless times she'd suffered the humiliation of skinned knees coupled with Priscilla's demonstrative sigh made her change the subject. 'Is the estate in financial difficulties?' she asked, even as she knew it wasn't any of her business.

'Whatever gave you that idea? Did Tom say that?' Priscilla tilted her chin and looked down her slim, elegant nose.

'Tom didn't say very much at all.'

Priscilla sighed again. 'Well, naturally it's expensive to run an estate like this. Stonybrook is a national heritage and has to be safeguarded for future generations. So yes, we have to be careful. Which reminds me, we recently had to let one of the ladies serving in the café go, so when you're not busy, perhaps you could make yourself useful over there.'

The words were delivered with a coquettish smile, but the steely look in Priscilla's blue eyes told Justine she was being put in her place. Not that she minded helping out; Rexus didn't demand around-the-clock care, and she'd rather be busy than not. It would help combat the feeling of loneliness that had begun to creep over her.

But it still rankled.

'Of course,' she said. 'I'll do whatever is necessary.'

Priscilla smiled again, and a snake would have looked friendlier. 'I'm glad we understand each other. And, by the way, you need to be wary of Tom. The last thing he needs is someone else to mess up his life.'

Oh yes, they understood each other just fine; Justine was being kept out of the way in a Cinderella-like existence because Priscilla didn't want any competition for the male attention, or for the position as first lady, but it puzzled Justine that Priscilla should think she had any plans in that direction.

It didn't matter. She'd settle Rexus, and then she was out of here, handsome, red-haired groundsmen notwithstanding.

4

Tom met her at Rexus's enclosure the next morning. Frost was in the air, and his cheeks were red from the cold which, combined with his auburn hair, gave him a fresh-faced, eager look.

'Good morning,' he said. 'Happy with the grub I gave him earlier?'

Justine nodded. 'The main thing is that Rexus is happy, and he seems to be.'

'Good.' He paused, suddenly uncertain. 'Remember I said I would show you around today?'

What was it with this guy? First he didn't want her here, and now he wanted to give her the guided tour . . . But she was in too good a mood to remind him, and instead she said, 'Sure, I remember. But only if you have time. And I'm supposed to be helping out in the café. Priscilla asked me yesterday.'

'You mean, demanded?'

'Pretty much.'

Tom grinned, and his confidence seemed to return. 'Priscilla is good at delegating, especially the jobs she considers beneath herself. Anyway, the café doesn't open until ten, so that gives you a couple of hour's free time.'

'I thought the lady of the house didn't have to do anything other than look decorative.' She knew that sounded bitchy, but Priscilla's attitude had really annoyed her.

'You'd be surprised at how much work is involved in running an estate, even a modest one like Stonybroke. Priscilla is good at the whole social thing, like organising village fetes and judging homemade jams and that kind of thing. Although I think she'd prefer looking decorative. And shopping.'

So, not that bitchy? 'Stony*broke*?'

'Brook,' he corrected. 'But you guessed it. The estate is fairly broke.'

'How can it be only fairly broke? Either it is or it isn't.'

'Oh, there is money, but the old man, I mean Lord Brooks, is keeping a tight grip on it.'

'So Henry is heir to a lot of financial trouble?'

'No, Henry isn't the heir. He's only the steward. The old man wanted it to go to Henry's uncle Edward but — '

'But?'

'Edward is dead. Died in a car accident, caught by a fast-moving flood tide out on the coast years ago. His family too.'

'Why is Henry not the heir then?'

'The old man is a little, uhm, idiosyncratic, and he doesn't like Priscilla.'

Who does, thought Justine uncharitably.

'On top of that Edward's body was never found. In fact, none of the bodies were ever found, and I suspect the old man is hoping that one of them is alive. He refuses to believe Edward is gone. It's complicated.'

Justine grinned. 'Sounds like it.'

Tom shrugged. 'Personally I don't think Edward would've walked away from all this. Why would he?'

With a sweeping gesture Tom indicated the parkland around them, the lawn with the weeping willows, the swans cruising silently on the lake, the forested area beyond the lake. A pair of robins flew down from a tree to sit on the grass a little away from them, and in the distance Justine heard the sharp cry of a fox.

Idyllic and tranquil were the first words that came into her mind, then expansive and fresh with a strange promise in the crisp air like nothing she'd ever experienced before. As much as she loved the hustle and bustle of circus life, a curious feeling of happiness bubbled in her stomach as she breathed, *really* breathed for the first time in her life. If Tom hadn't been standing right next to her, she would have spread her arms wide and twirled around on the spot, laughing.

He was right. How could anyone

want to give this up? She wanted to say so, to share with him this unexpected exhilaration that still fluttered in her chest, but self-consciousness got the better of her, and instead she let him lead the way to where he was planning on taking her.

They crossed the lawn to the set of outbuildings on the other side of the estate away from where her flat was. 'Where do you fit in?' she asked. 'I mean, in the inheritance stakes.'

'I don't,' Tom replied. 'Henry and I are first cousins. His mother and mine are sisters.'

'And Henry's father?'

'Died of cancer many years ago. Henry's mum remarried and now lives in Spain. Losing both his sons is another reason the old man has become extra stubborn. It's made him a bit doolally, I fear. Actually, that's not fair,' he added as he pushed open the gate to another courtyard. 'There's nothing wrong with his mind, just his judgment.' He held the gate open for Justine.

'Thank you,' she murmured, but Tom seemed suddenly distant.

'I call him the old man because Henry refers to him that way, and because he isn't my grandfather. But he sometimes behaves like a grandfather to me, like when I was going through a rough patch. Both he and Henry came through for me.'

'Frankly, your family tree is a complete mystery to me,' Justine replied, to lighten the mood.

She succeeded. Tom laughed. 'Then, let's not worry about that any more. Come, I want you to meet Coco and Homer.'

He opened the door to one of the outbuildings. 'These are the newer stables, of course. The other stables have been converted into a café, the one where you'll be helping out.'

'I know.'

'You know?' Tom sent her a questioning look.

'Well, they look new.'

'Yep. Only about twenty years or so. Anyway, we don't have many animals, just these two, the cat belonging to the girls, and the hyenas and the porcupine, which the old man rescued from another private zoo.'

A soft nickering greeted them, and a chestnut gelding stuck his nose out of a bay. 'This is Homer, named after the Greek epic poet, and *not* Homer Simpson. And this is Coco,' he added as a smaller, black horse appeared in the next bay. 'She's named after Coco Chanel. My wife's idea, and the only thing she didn't lay claim to after our divorce, apart from personal belongings. The old man kindly lets me keep them here.'

The last he added as if to himself, and Justine didn't comment. Priscilla had said something about Tom not needing someone else to mess up his life, and this must be what she'd meant.

Absurdly pleased that she'd still be around horses, if only for another few weeks, she stroked the mare's bristly mane. Dark, gentle eyes met hers. 'Hello, Coco.'

The horse blew softly out of her nose.

'She likes you,' said Tom. 'Normally she's a bit skittish around strangers.'

'I'm used to horses, so that's probably why.'

'Of course you are.' Tom grinned. 'I'd forgotten for a moment. I expect you're used to all sorts of things. I imagine you must have lived a very varied life, certainly more than most people your age.'

Justine leaned into Coco, breathing in the familiar horsey scent.

'I suppose so.' She sighed, remembering suddenly that life as she'd always known it was over. Last night, in the flat above the garages, she'd eaten on her own for the first time in . . . well, forever. So oppressive was the silence that she'd hardly tasted the fresh pasta and expensive organic tomato sauce, which some kind person had left for her in the fridge.

Tom fed Homer a sugar lump. 'What will you do now that the circus has closed down? I mean, after we've settled the lion.'

'I don't know,' she replied. 'I won't be able to work with big cats in England, and I don't fancy going abroad. The sensible thing would be to refine my wire-walking act and join a new circus next season.'

'Well, if there's anything I can do to help you practise, let me know.'

'I will.'

They said goodbye to the horses, and Tom took her to see more of the estate; the dovecote, the greenhouse where the old man, he explained, liked to potter around on his own, and then the edge of the woods.

'Tell me about your life at the circus,' said Tom.

'Sheesh!' Justine laughed. 'How long have you got? It's like asking someone to explain a complicated mathematical question in a couple of minutes. We live together, and we work together. There's often long days of rehearsal, tending animals, repairing costumes, checking equipment, things like that. This is when we're not performing because when we *are* performing, you just add that on top of it.'

'Don't you ever have any free time?'

Justine thought for a moment. 'Sure, but we tend to spend that together, one way or another. After a performance it's quite common for us to eat together.'

As the memories of a less complicated life flooded back, she could almost smell the barbecue her mother and the rest of the catering staff would light on the back lot. Then all the kids would run, skip or jump, balancing their plates and hoping to be the first in the queue for Beth's renowned burgers. When daylight faded, the men and the boys would light bonfires to keep the mosquitoes at bay, and someone might pluck the strings of a guitar or play oldies on the radio. The perfect end to a perfect day.

But it was hard to put this into words so Tom would understand.

'It's quite noisy and chaotic,' she said

instead. 'Like an extended family. I remember a performer from a Scandinavian country whose family travelled with the circus for a couple of seasons, a teenager like I was at the time, well, anyway he used to refer to his circus family as 'the hunchbacks' because he saw them as one big, lumpen and misshapen unit.'

'Hmm, not terribly PC, is it?' Tom said.

'I know but I rather like it.' Justine smiled. 'I'm a seventh generation circus performer, and this is how we live. It's all I've ever known, all these personalities, the ideas and the energy surrounding us.'

She told Tom about her cousin Janos who would always clown around, even outside the ring. Gentle Gabi, whom Tom had already met, and his love of horses; Sara, petite and ethereal, Yolande with her thick accent and lithe physique. Her parents who always held hands when they thought no one was looking, Uncle Jethro who could shout down the mountains which was why he was MC. And so many others, even all the animals, all part of the same life.

'That's how we lot lice live. I just can't imagine life any other way.'

'*Lot lice*?' Tom raised an eyebrow.

'The children who grow up on the back lot, which is the area between the caravans. It's kind of like, uhm . . . ' Justine paused as she searched for the right word.

'A village?'

'Yes, like a travelling village.'

'It sounds fun,' said Tom.

'It can be. It's hard work, and when it rains, it can be a bit of a drag, especially for the caterers like my mum. And the ones helping her. Meaning me. And now it's . . . ' She shrugged. What was there to add? Those days were gone for good.

'But you can find another circus, though, can't you?' Tom asked.

'Oh, most likely. Like I said, I need to perfect my own act. The wire-walking,' she added in response to Tom's questioning look.

'I thought you had that down to a tee.'

'What made you think that?' Justine hadn't shown him any tricks.

'The way you walk,' he replied. 'Always in a straight line. I bet you could fool a drunk-driving test!'

She laughed. 'I wouldn't even think about it. Bad stuff happens when people drink and drive.' Perhaps that was what had happened to Henry's uncle, Edward, the one who drove into the sea. A sad thought. She changed the subject. 'When my father disbanded the circus, he told me it was time for me to go my own way, and he was right. At Belmont I spent most of my time helping my parents, my father with the cats and my mother with the catering, and my own act was always brief because I only have a few tricks. For a few seasons I performed with a well-known international wire-walker who toured with us, but I was merely the eye candy. Truth be told, I'm not sure I was ever that good in the first place. I need to think of some new tricks, study other artists on YouTube and find a way of making them uniquely mine.'

'Well, as I said before, if there's anything I can do to help . . . Do you have a laptop with you?'

'I have my smartphone.'

'In that case you're welcome to use the computer in my office, just down the corridor from the kitchen. The password is 'stonybroke', no capital letters. And don't worry, there's nothing sensitive or private on there as Henry does the finances.'

'Thanks, I might do that.'

They had reached the forested area on the other side of the lake. On the edge of it stood two enormous cedar trees, the branches heavy with clusters of cones. Judging by the height of them, Justine thought they must be at least a hundred years old. Behind them lay the trunk of the same kind of tree, cut down probably due to disease and perhaps left there for something to sit on.

Or to balance on. Justine imagined

Henry's two girls doing just that when their mother wasn't watching.

She had a sudden idea. Touching one of the reddish brown trunks, she turned to Tom. 'You said you wanted to help me. Would it be possible to place a wire between these two trees, about two to three feet off the ground? I know I won't be here for more than a few weeks, but I could then get started on some new acts, and afterwards maybe Henry's daughters could play here. They seemed a little bored.'

'That's a very good idea,' said Tom. 'I'll look into it straight away. Should be able to get some suitable materials from the local DIY store. As for the girls, I couldn't say. That's exclusively Priscilla's department.'

Exactly what Justine had thought, and she stopped herself just in time before she said something derogatory about Priscilla's parenting style. It took all sorts, and because she herself had had a particular upbringing, it didn't give her the right to judge someone else. Still, there was something in the way Priscilla had watched her which grated on her nerves.

'Thank you,' she said instead. Under the evergreen canopy of the cedars she caught Tom's smile. Leaning into the trunk of the tree, she found herself holding his green-eyed gaze for longer than perhaps was necessary, then she turned away and looked back across the lake towards the house.

Excited as she was at the prospect of developing a few new acts and a new season in a familiar environment, it would be difficult to leave Stonybrook again. If ever she imagined a place other than the circus where she could put down roots, it would be here.

And not just because of Rexus.

* * *

When she entered the café in the disused stables later, Justine was immediately enveloped by warmth and the smell of baking.

There were no customers at the moment, but she pictured them stomping their feet and rubbing their hands against the cold outside, having been enticed indoors to spend their hard-earned cash on proprietary teas and home-made cakes after a bracing stroll in the park. Tom certainly knew what he was doing.

The nod to the festive season was more understated here, with sprigs of holly in little jugs on each of the tables and what looked like hand-knitted bunting in red, white and green festooning the walls and the old stable bays. A stark contrast to the opulence of the family's lounge.

'Oh, there you are. You must be the circus girl.'

The woman in charge handed Justine a dark green apron with a white outline of Stonybrook on the front. She wore a similar apron and had tied her light brown hair back in a perky ponytail. Her hazel eyes twinkled with humour.

'I'm Dawn by the way. And you are

Justine, I think? Love the name. Wish my parents had had the imagination to give me something a bit more fancy like that. But, no, my sisters and I all have really ordinary names.'

Her flow of words made Justine a little breathless; circus people tended to talk less when they worked because it broke concentration.

'Dawn is a pretty name,' she said.

'Aww, aren't you lovely?' Dawn gave her a squeeze. 'Now, how are you with making scones?'

'Okay, I think.' Justine often helped her mother with the catering, and although an oven in a caravan was rarely big, you could make enough if you used other people's ovens as well.

'Great, fantastic!' Dawn led the way to the kitchen through a swing door behind the café counter. 'The lady who normally makes them for us has the flu, and people who come here do like a good cream tea. It's kind of our signature dish, if you like.'

Dawn crooked her fingers in the air,

then began pulling ingredients out of a massive cupboard and put them on a stainless steel kitchen island. 'And here's a recipe in case you need it. We open in half an hour. Should be enough time for scones, but we aren't usually overrun with customers until about eleven anyway. I'll be out front arranging cakes.'

She left through the swing door, and Justine wasted no time in mixing the dough and getting a large batch of scones in the oven. She was used to cooking with an electric oven, when she wasn't using a barbeque, but working with gas turned out to be easier than she'd expected.

In fact, it was an absolute joy, and she hummed to herself as she took in her surroundings. The kitchen was at one end of the old stable, and had incorporated the old horse stalls as useful storage in such a way that they became a feature. An old manger ran along the wall, and the cobbled flooring in the bays themselves had been maintained, while the main pedestrian areas were quarry tiled.

Justine could almost hear the clanking of the harnesses, the gentle snorting of the horses as they stomped contently while munching their hay. The image was as vivid as if she'd been there.

A deep voice pulled her back to reality. 'Mm, something smells nice.'

Tom had entered the kitchen through a door at the other end, trailing cold air behind him, and was rubbing his hands to warm them.

'Scones,' she said.

'I didn't know you could bake. I thought you could only tame lions and line-dance.'

'Only?' She arched her brows. 'Trust me, I'm an-all-rounder. You have to muck in at the circus.'

'That's what I like to hear.'

'Really? Which part? Being an all-rounder or mucking in?'

'Both,' he said and held her eyes for a brief moment. 'I'm not into girls who have grand ideas of their own importance and consider themselves above giving a hand.'

'Are you into me, then?' The words flew out of her mouth before she realised it. According to Priscilla, Tom wasn't into women at all.

'Yes, well, no. I mean . . . ' He reddened and turned away.

Just as well because Justine's own face had suddenly gone hot. She grabbed an oven mitten and tested the scones.

'These are ready if you fancy one. You can be my guinea pig.' She handed Tom a scone hot from the oven and fetched strawberry jam and clotted cream from the fridge, then to cover up her own embarrassment, she said, 'I was thinking earlier how strange it was to bake scones, or do any kind of baking for that matter, in what used to be a smelly stable.'

'Not so smelly now. Horses haven't lived in here for many years.'

'I know.'

'You know? How come?'

'Because you told me earlier today.'

'Ah yes, well, the stables were considered unsuitable according to modern standards, I'm told. And now only Coco and Homer live in the new stables.'

Justine nodded.

'Do you ride?' Tom asked suddenly.

'Well, durr! I grew up in a circus, of course I ride.'

He laughed. 'Then we'll go riding sometime when neither of us are busy. Deal?'

'Deal.'

Tom finished his scone. 'Delicious. Almost as good as the ones the woman in the village bakes for us.'

Justine flicked flour and crumbs at him that she'd been cleaning up. 'Almost? Tch.'

'I take it back. They're better than the other ones.' He brushed the crumbs from his sleeve. 'Anyway, I came to tell you that I've been to the ironmonger's and bought a wire and some adjustable brackets. I'm just off to fit it now. Do you have any specific requirements?'

Justine shook her head. 'Only the height we discussed. Two to three feet above the ground.'

'Yes, I remember.' His face suddenly cracked into a cheeky grin. 'I look forward to watching you practise.'

'Don't you dare! I'll be totally self-conscious if you do.'

'Yeah? I would've thought you'd be used to people looking at you.'

'This is different,' she said.

'Why?' he pressed.

She shrugged. 'I don't know. I . . . '

'Well, when you figure it out, you let me know. Catch you later.' He winked at her and left the way he'd come.

Justine crossed her arms. Now, what to make of that? It was almost as if he was flirting with her, really flirting. But what was the point? She was leaving in few weeks, off to pastures new, and he knew that.

Was he perhaps trying to make her stay more enjoyable? She could deal with that. A little harmless flirtation never hurt anyone.

5

The next morning was slightly hazy, and the air had the kind of dampness to it that seemed to seep into a person's bones. Nevertheless the weather had never stopped Justine from doing what she needed to do, and she went to collect the bucket of meat for Rexus, which she'd left to defrost overnight in one of the old garages which was being used as the café's food storage.

A frustrated roar greeted her when she was halfway across the lawn. The youngest of Henry's two daughters, the one named Cordelia, had climbed through the spectator barrier and was teasing Rexus by running a stick along the fencing creating a deafening clatter while the other girl looked on.

Justine dropped the bucket of meat and in a few strides she reached the enclosure and snatched the stick out of the girl's hand, then bundled her back onto the other side of the barrier.

'What do you think you're doing?' she shouted. 'This is a lion!'

'I just wanted to play with him.' Cordelia's lip wobbled at Justine's harsh words.

'You have no right to talk to my sister in that way,' said the older girl Portia, her pert little nose in the air. 'You're nothing but the hired help.'

'The hired help, huh? If it comes to teaching two rude children a well-deserved lesson, I can certainly help with that!'

'You can't teach us anything. We go to a private school. I bet you can't even read or write.' Portia's nose stuck further in the air so the girl was in danger of toppling backwards. Her cut-glass accent, so like her mother's, grated on Justine's ears.

This was too absurd, and Justine laughed. 'Is that so? Well, I'd wager I know a thing or two they don't teach you at your fine school.'

'Done.' Portia's haughty expression

was replaced by a cheeky grin, and she stuck out her hand. 'A fiver, and we shake on it.'

'I can do better than that.' Justine spat in the palm of her hand and presented it to Portia. The girl hesitated for a moment, then she did the same, and they shook hands.

'But I still think I might be cleverer than you,' she said.

'Oh, I don't doubt it.' Justine's tone was dry. 'I only went to school during the winter when the circus season ended.'

'Only in the winter?' Cordelia cut in. 'That's so unfair!'

'Guess I was lucky. Now, about Rexus, you can't play with lions, not the way you play with a cat.'

Cordelia pouted. 'But Daddy says they're just like big cats.'

'They're part of the cat family, yes, but they're big and strong. Your cat might scratch your hand if it gets excited, but a lion could rip your stomach open. And then you'd die.'

Cordelia's face fell, and she burst

into tears. Portia put her arm around her younger sister.

'You've frightened her now.'

'Fear isn't a bad thing if it teaches a person to be careful.' Justine was still angry and shocked at what Cordelia had been doing, but she softened a little at the sight of the girl's obvious distress. And no one had come to any harm.

'Rexus can be a little frightened too, you know.' She indicated the enclosure. 'This is all new to him. For as long as he can remember, he's lived in a cage about the size of a small garage and only been let out when he was in the arena and had to work. And there were other animals nearby. But now he's all alone in this big space with only those sleepy hyenas next door, and he's not quite sure what to do with himself.'

Cordelia dried her eyes with a dirty little hand, streaking her face with grime. 'Rexus is afraid?'

'Well, he's definitely a little uncertain about everything. And when animals are frightened, they either run away or lash out.'

'So what can we do to make him feel better?' Portia asked.

'First of all, we don't tease him,' Justine replied firmly.

Cordelia nodded.

'Then we have to behave in a calm way around him. Not shout or cry but just talk in a soothing voice, like I'm doing right now.' Subconsciously she'd lowered the pitch of her voice as she always did around animals.

'I can do that,' said Portia. 'Dilly?'

'Yes,' Cordelia half-whispered.

'Then what do we do?' Portia insisted.

'It's great what you're doing, and try to remember it around all kinds of animals. Unless you have to give them a command like telling a dog to 'sit' perhaps. Then you can be a bit more forceful.'

'We understand. Don't we, Dilly?'

Cordelia nodded again, enthusiastically and with new-found confidence.

'There's no 'we' about it with Rexus,' said Justine. 'Only someone trained to be around big cats should approach a lion, and only someone the lion trusts. It can take years to build up that trust. Basically you have to know him from a baby.'

'So we can't go in there and stroke him even if you go with us?' Cordelia asked.

'Definitely not! You must never do that. Promise me? Anyway, it's locked, so you can't go in.'

'I know where the key is,' said Portia, her nose reaching the skies again triumphantly.

You would, wouldn't you? Justine glared at her. Too smart for her own good, that kid.

'But I won't use it,' said Portia.

'Good. What we *can* do is to get him used to your individual smells. Dilly, could I borrow your scarf for a moment? Or do you have a pair of gloves in your coat pocket?'

Dilly handed her a woollen mitten with a Fair Isle pattern, and Justine climbed through the barrier and approached the chain link fence. Rexus, who'd wandered off to sit on a large boulder, turned when she called him.

'Rexus. Come on, big boy!'

'Nngh,' the lion grunted, swishing his plume-tipped tail from side to side.

'Rexus,' Justine called again and dangled Cordelia's glove in front of the fence.

The lion grunted again but curiosity got the better of him and he ventured back to the fence. Justine held up her hand for him to sniff, close enough to the fencing so he could smell her but not quite touching it as Rexus still appeared irritated.

The lion gave a series of low grunts as he recognised her personal smell in the still unfamiliar environment. Justine then held up Cordelia's mitten, which he sniffed cautiously, then recoiled a little.

'It's okay, baby, she didn't mean it.' Justine put the glove a little closer, and Rexus sniffed it again, made another guttural sound, then lay down on the ground and rolled from side to side a few times. Justine returned to the other side of the barrier and handed the mitten back to Cordelia.

'What does that mean?' Portia asked.

'He's happy. He's smelled Dilly and knows now that she's not a threat to him. We'll do the same thing tomorrow, and with something of yours as well, Portia. A step at a time with Rexus. He's had enough for now.' Justine smiled wryly at the absurdity of sweet little Cordelia being a threat to anyone, let alone a lion.

'Does that mean he won't eat me?' Cordelia asked.

'He can't if you don't go in there, and you promised me you wouldn't.'

'I won't!' Cordelia replied, a little wide-eyed at the idea.

'The thing about cats, even small ones, is that they're predators. Hunters,' Justine added when Cordelia looked confused. 'They hunt their food, that's what keeps them active. Even your house cat. What's it called?'

'Tibbie,' said Portia. 'He's a boy.

Dilly always pulls his tail. I tell her not to but she never listens.'

'And you dress him in your dolly's clothes!' Cordelia countered.

'I don't play with dolls anymore.'

Justine laughed. 'I bet he absolutely hates that.'

'He growls,' Portia admitted.

'That's his way of saying he doesn't like it. Animals obviously can't talk like we do so it's our job to look at how they're acting and figure out what they're trying to tell us. And right now I think Rexus actually wants his breakfast, and it's probably best if you step back a little. When he smells meat, he can get a little possessive because he doesn't want to share with anyone.'

The girls nodded. 'But we can still watch, can't we?'

'Sure.'

'Can we put Christmas decorations up on the cage later?' asked Cordelia.

Justine shook her head. 'I don't think that's such a good idea. They might frighten him.'

'And we must never frighten him.' Cordelia nodded sagely.

'No.'

'What *exactly* is going on here?' Priscilla had come up behind them and grabbed both girls by the arm. 'You're not to go anywhere near that animal, do you hear? And why are you so filthy, Cordelia? I'm really disappointed in your behaviour.' She turned to Justine. 'Is this your influence?'

'No, she — ' Portia began.

'I thought the girls would like to see Rexus being fed so I asked them to come with me.'

'But — ' Portia said, but Justine shook her head slightly.

'I wasn't aware they weren't allowed here. I'm sorry about that.'

'No, they're certainly *not* allowed here without supervision!'

Without supervision? What am I, then? Justine thought but let it go. She wasn't staying at Stonybrook for long, and life was too short for unnecessary conflict.

'I'd appreciate it if you'd refrain from interfering with the girls' upbringing in the future,' Priscilla snapped. 'Come along, you two. We're going into town. We need to get you a new winter coat, Portia.'

'But I like the one I've got.'

'It's a year old. Fashions change.'

'I don't care about fashion.' Portia's shoulders slumped.

'Nonsense, all girls do,' said Priscilla mildly and took both her daughters by the hand, more gently this time. 'Now, if you'll excuse us,' she said over her shoulder to Justine. 'I expect you have things to do as well.'

'Helping out in the café, yes.'

'Of course.' With that Priscilla left, half-dragging the reluctant Portia with her.

Justine watched them leave, pensive. This was so different from the way she'd been brought up. Not that her parents couldn't afford things — circus people were generally well paid — there just hadn't been time for shopping as a recreational activity, only when you really needed something.

Shaking her head, she fetched the bucket of meat she'd dropped earlier, unlocked the gate to the enclosure, and went in to feed Rexus.

* * *

Later in the day after she'd done her stint at the café, she sought out Tom and found him in his office tapping away at the computer keyboard. He looked up and sent her a beaming smile when he spotted her in the doorway.

'Knock, knock,' she said.

'Come in. My door is always open to you. Actually, my door is always open, full stop, but it's nice to see you.'

'Yeah, about that — '

'Sorry about the mess.' Distracted, Tom rose and moved a teetering pile of papers from a chair opposite his desk to a filing cabinet full of other teetering piles, thus making whatever mess he was apologising for even worse.

Justine smiled. She didn't mind the mess; it was sort of homely, and if Tom knew where everything was, then who was she to comment?

'Please, sit down,' he said. 'I can make you some coffee if you like.'

'It's okay, you don't have to.'

'Oh, I insist. Gives me an excuse to use this fancy thingummyjig my parents gave me as an early Christmas present. Trouble is, I don't know how to work it.'

He pointed to a shiny, bright red coffee maker on the windowsill behind him next to a small fibre optic Christmas tree which had been plugged in and was cycling through various colours: blue, red, purple, white. Justine smiled at the tackiness of the tree; it was so like the one they used to have in the caravan.

'I do,' said Justine. 'Would you like me to show you?'

He grinned. 'Please.'

Justine stepped around his desk and showed him how to load the little pods, how to empty the holder with discarded pods when full, where to fill up with water, which Tom did from a water filter he kept in a small fridge in the office, and how to use the milk foamer. All the while she was conscious of his nearness, his body heat, and that particular smell of fresh air and horses that she'd come to associate with him. So like the circus.

She wondered what would happen if she were to slide her arm around him, just to check that he was real, but pushed the idea aside almost immediately. Why send signals that she was available when she really wasn't?

To hide her thoughts she wrapped her hands around her mug and enjoyed the pleasant aroma of freshly brewed coffee. Tom had a way of making her forget herself.

'Aren't you a star?' he said when they were sitting down, safely on either side of the desk.

Justine shrugged. 'As I've told you before, I'm an all-rounder.'

'Well, a girl who can operate a convoluted coffee machine wins my heart.'

She blushed and blew the milk foam across the top of her mug. 'It's not that difficult,' she muttered.

Perhaps sensing that he'd said more than he should have, Tom cleared his throat. 'I saw you with Henry's girls earlier, by the enclosure. You seemed to be telling them off for something, and I didn't want to interfere. God knows, they could do with it from time to time!'

'Oh yes, that. Cordelia had climbed under the barrier and was running a stick along the fence, upsetting Rexus. I didn't think it was a good idea to piss off a lion and told them so.'

'Quite.' Tom frowned.

'I put the key back in your office. I expect you found it.'

'I saw it on its peg.'

'I actually came to talk to you about that. Portia knows where the key is kept, and it might be a good idea to put it somewhere else. Just in case.'

'You don't trust her?'

'In a word, no. She's a mischief-maker, that one, but going into a lion's den is no joke. And I think we need to nail some chicken wire to those wooden posts. At the moment it's just too tempting for a child to slip through the gap and go right up to the fence. People would still be able to climb it, but they might think twice. The extra barrier is there for a reason.'

Tom nodded, his frown even deeper. 'I'll move the key to somewhere safer and let you know. And I'll secure the barrier this afternoon. Thanks for telling me. The girls are naughty, but not stupid. I've spoken to Henry before about what they get up to, but he doesn't seem to take it seriously. And it's no use talking to Priscilla. I'll have another word with him.'

Justine nodded, and they finished their coffee without speaking. The silence hung above them, full of things unsaid. Tom seemed genuinely fond of his second cousins or whatever they were; the complicated family history still boggled her mind. And he seemed maybe a little bit fond of her as well despite his supposed aversion to women.

So, what are you going to do about it? she thought.

Nothing. Absolutely nothing.

⋆ ⋆ ⋆

To banish the images of Tom and his homely office from her mind, Justine decided to look in on Rexus before going to bed. Holding a torch she'd borrowed from Tom's workshop, she made her way across the lawn to the lion's enclosure, the frosty grass crunching under her boots.

The nocturnal porcupine in the smallest of the cages was now wide awake and munching away at slices of butternut squash which Tom must have left for it earlier just inside the fence. It didn't appear bothered by the cone of light from the torch, and its high-pitched contented noises, a cross between a whiny dog and a kazoo, Justine thought, echoed in the still evening air.

Four pinpricks of light told her that the hyenas were awake too, and watching her silently. A shiver ran down her spine. She'd never liked hyenas and the cackling sound they made, their too calculating and too untameable nature, but she knew they were excellent hunters, and that in the wild lions often stole the prey hyenas had brought down. Which sort of went against her sense of fairness.

'I haven't got anything for you,' she muttered. 'Sorry.'

The four lights vanished as the hyenas turned their backs on her.

She started slightly at the shadow in front of the lion's cage. Her first thought was Tom, and she experienced an annoying flutter in her chest — she was trying to get away from the man! — but this person was shorter and a little stooped.

Lord Brooks.

'Hello,' she said when she stopped beside him. Rexus sat just on the other side of the fence, sphinx-like with his front legs flat on the ground, as if he was studying the man studying him.

Lord Brooks nodded curtly but kept his eyes on the lion. 'Magnificent beast, isn't he?'

Pride swelled in Justine's chest. 'He is.'

'Settling in well?'

'He seems to be,' she replied. 'I don't think I'll need to impose on your hospitality for much longer.'

Lord Brooks harrumphed dismissively. 'Don't trouble yourself about that. The place is big enough.'

'I suppose.'

He turned sharply and faced her for the first time. 'And you? What do you think of Stonybroke?' He gave a gruff laugh. 'Yes, I know what Tom calls it. Cheeky runt.'

Justine laughed at the thought of Tom as the runt of the litter. His height and athletic build made him the exact opposite.

'Well?'

'It's . . . it's beautiful here,' she replied. 'You're very lucky.'

'Yes,' he said in a tone that suggested the subject bored him, and turned his eyes back on the lion. 'Lucky, indeed.'

They stood for a moment in silence just looking at Rexus who grunted contentedly at their presence, then Lord Brooks retrieved a cane which he'd hung from its handle on the wooden barrier. 'Best be heading back before the lady of the house sends out a search party. I'm not supposed to be out of bed at this hour, you see.'

Even in the sparse light Justine caught the twinkle in his eyes. 'Would you like me to walk with you?'

'No, thank you. I know the way.'

He turned abruptly and lifted his hand in a lazy wave. Justine stared after him until the darkness swallowed him up.

What a peculiar old fellow. But peculiar in a nice way.

6

Preparations for Priscilla's annual Christmas party started on the twenty-second of December. Justine had been at Stonybrook for little over a week, and had helped out in the café every day. Rexus seemed more settled in his new surroundings although bored, and to alleviate his boredom she decided to make him something to play with, which would also keep his mind sharp.

In one of the many outbuildings she found some rope and an old plank of wood that Tom said he didn't need. She sawed the plank into five medium-sized pieces of wood and drilled a hole in each for the rope to pass through. Then she painted the numbers '1' to '5' on them.

Back at the enclosure she climbed an oak tree adjacent to the animal pen, from which a long branch jutted out over the enclosure, providing shade and natural shelter for the animals. It was high enough that no large cat would be able to reach it by jumping up, and certainly not an aged lion like Rexus.

Rexus grunted and rolled on the ground beneath the branch as Justine tied the five lengths of rope to the branch, then climbed down again as he started playing with the suspended pieces of wood with his giant paw.

The girls and Henry had come up to the enclosure while Justine was climbing the tree. Eagerness mixed with guilt showed on their faces.

'I thought I'd take the girls to say hello to the lion,' said Henry. 'They begged me, and I thought it would be all right with me to supervise them. And Priscilla is busy, so . . . '

He gave a little shrug, his cheeks flushed. Plainly his wife had other ideas about him being here. Cordelia was clutching her father's hand; perhaps she remembered Justine's warning about Rexus. She hoped so.

'It's okay. I won't tell.' She grinned, and Henry smiled back.

'Can he really do maths?' Portia asked. 'We saw him at the circus when we were on holiday.'

I remember, Justine nearly said, but it had been Tom she remembered, and also that she'd mistaken the girls for being *his* daughters.

'Well, not really. At least I don't think so. It's actually a trick. See those pieces of wood? They're not hung at exactly the same height, and what Rexus would normally do would be to watch my father's cane, like a pointer.'

'But in the circus it was blocks, not things hanging down,' Portia pointed out.

'The principle is the same. Rexus watches the lion-tamer, not the blocks. And sometimes we hang numbered boards like these ones in his cage to stop him getting bored.'

'So, he's not clever?' Cordelia asked, still staying very close to her father.

'Oh yes, he's a clever animal. He has

to watch very carefully, and it's hard enough for people to see what my father does. Even more so for a lion.'

'Fascinating,' said Henry. 'Would you indulge us, please?'

'You mean, make Rexus perform?'

He smiled. 'If it's not too much trouble. Or too dangerous,' he added, 'although he seems a congenial beast.'

'It's no trouble, but . . . ' Justine hesitated. 'I'm not my father, and I don't know if he'll respond to me in the same way.'

She'd thought of trying to work with Rexus herself, mainly to keep him entertained, except not in front of an audience. But Henry's smile was so pleasant and quietly insisting, and the girls looked so eager. Even if it didn't quite work, it could do no harm and would teach the girls a different kind of respect for the lion.

Making her mind up, she fetched a bamboo cane she'd found leaning up against the outside of Lord Brooks's greenhouse — which Tom had told her was off-limits — and unlocked the enclosure. Rexus was lying sphinx-like with his paws out in front of him, but got up as if he'd guessed what was about to happen. With the cane in her hand Justine approached the suspended wood pieces and pointed to number 1 and number 2.

'One plus two, Rexus.'

The lion stared intently at the numbers, but Justine knew he was following the subtle movements she made with the cane, which she now held level with the bottom edge of the number 3.

Rexus grunted, then shook his mane and scratched himself lazily behind one ear with his back leg.

'Come on, Rexus. You can do it. One plus two.'

She pointed to the numbers again. Rexus yawned, revealing his large yellow teeth and long tongue, then got up and sauntered off to the other end of the enclosure.

Turning to Henry and the girls,

Justine shook her head. 'It's not working, I'm afraid.'

'What a shame,' said Henry. 'Another time, perhaps.'

The girls' shoulders slumped and Justine had a sudden idea. 'Listen, I'll try something else. I've never done this before, and it may confuse him even more, but it's worth a try.'

She left the enclosure, locking the gate securely behind her. She caught Portia's eye as she dropped the key back in her pocket, but Portia quickly looked away again. She was glad she'd talked to Tom about moving the key; now only the two of them knew where it was kept.

Taking off her shoes and socks, she climbed the tree again, this time walking the length of the branch as she would a circus wire. The air was cold on her feet at first, but she'd always been blessed with good circulation and soon warmed up. Using her toes to balance on the branch, she sauntered over to where she'd tied the ropes with the numbers earlier. With her cane she touched the numbers 1 and 2 as before, making them sway slightly in the air.

'One plus two,' she said again.

Curiosity got the better of the lion, and Rexus came back and sat underneath the branch looking up. His dark eyes darted between the swaying pieces of board, then up at Justine, waiting for his cue. Surreptitiously she curled up her big toe on the side of the branch nearest the number 3, and Rexus pawed the right piece, then rolled on the ground, pleased with himself when Justine praised him.

'Goodness me,' said Henry, when she'd climbed down from the tree and joined the others again. 'I don't know what you did there, but I didn't spot it.'

'It was your toe, wasn't it?' said Portia.

Justine nodded. 'You have sharp eyes. Yes, I used my toe, but at the circus the audience looks at the lion not the handler, and that's how we get away with it.'

'Well, I think it's frightfully clever!' Henry enthused, pleasant as always. 'And now we must be going. My wife will be wondering where we've got to.'

'There's Mummy.' Cordelia pointed across the lawn at Priscilla coming towards them. The girls ran to meet her, jumping up and down with excitement.

'Uh-oh,' Henry muttered under his breath, then smiled at Justine. 'I can see why my grandfather was drawn to the idea of having a lion here, although I'm still not sure where the money is going to come from to feed him and look after him. I don't suppose you've met my grandfather yet?'

'Only very briefly.'

'I'm sure you'll see more of him, at some point. He keeps different hours to the rest of us.'

Nodding goodbye, he went to meet his wife, who glared openly at Justine. Taking her hand, they walked back across the lawn to the house, a happy family by all accounts, which surprised Justine given Priscilla's controlling nature.

Portia looked back over her shoulder. Justine had praised the girl for her sharp eyes, and sharp they were. She hadn't missed a single movement when Justine had climbed the tree using a low-hanging branch to hoist herself up the first part of the trunk.

Another thing she needed to talk to Tom about; that branch presented a security hazard and had to come down. If she needed to, Justine would be able to swing herself up in other ways, but the girls wouldn't be tall enough to reach.

Still, she regretted her lack of caution; she should have known better where Portia was concerned.

* * *

Dawn and Justine were in the kitchen of Stonybrook putting the finishing touches to the multitude of different canapes Priscilla had requested they prepare for her Christmas party, when Tom came in. Justine hadn't seen him in a couple of days and seeing him now, so unexpectedly, brought a rush to her face. Icicles glittered in his red hair, and his cheeks had that habitual healthy outdoorsy glow.

'Here to sample the goods again?' she asked, her own cheeks flaming at the clumsy way she'd managed to phrase her question. Did he realise how handsome he was? Probably not.

'Don't mind if I do? What are all these different things? They look absolutely mouth-watering.'

His eyes lit up at the spread on display, and she had to admit it looked enticing. There was everything from pork and apricot, ham hock and spinach, Cheddar and bacon, chicken satay sticks with peanut sauce for dipping, mushroom and peperonata, mozzarella and olives, mini Margarita pizzas, and even little tubs of breaded fish with four or five hand-cut chips.

Faster than lightning, Tom wolfed down a selection of different canapes, and Dawn tutted.

'I swear that man can smell food

from a mile away.'

Tom grinned and licked his fingers. The unconscious gesture sent a thrill down Justine's spine. No man had ever had such a profound effect on her.

You've got it bad, she thought and busied herself rearranging the canapes to cover the empty spaces on the tray.

'Aren't you going to the party?' she asked. Tom was still wearing his rugged boots and a Barbour jacket that had seen better days, and the party was only ten minutes away.

'Oh, I'll put in an appearance, for the old man's sake. None of us are keen on this type of arrangement, but Priscilla likes for him to be there. Probably something to do with him being a baronet.' He winked at Justine, and she smiled back.

'Now you're just being nasty,' Dawn commented, with a twinkle in her eye. 'Couldn't possibly be the case.'

Tom laughed and turned back to Justine. 'I actually came to ask you if you'd like to join me and Richard for the Christingle service at the local church. It's always a very friendly and informal affair, and it puts one in the mood for Christmas. Sadly it clashed with Priscilla's party, but Richard isn't too fussed about that anyway.'

'I'd love to but . . . I'm not sure I'll have time.'

'Did Priscilla ask you to the party?' Tom looked so stunned that Justine laughed.

'Gosh no. I doubt if she'd want me there. She made it clear from the beginning that I'm not really welcome here, other than to work. I don't know what I might have done to upset her, but I tend to stay out of her way. Henry is very kind, though,' she added, in case Tom thought she was casting aspersions on his relatives.

'We all love Henry,' said Dawn. 'Not a bad bone in his body. But you should have time to go to the service. Priscilla has hired some local teenagers, including my daughter, to serve the canapes and champagne. Oh, the fuss that girl made when she realised she didn't have a black skirt! The required uniform, apparently, with a white shirt. This annual gig is so popular the kids are practically falling over themselves to get it.' Dawn wiped the edge of a tray with a tea towel where some peanut sauce had spilled out of the little dish. 'All you and I will have to do is to carry the trays into the anteroom next to the drawing room, and I'll supervise them.'

'If you're sure . . . ?'

'Of course I am.'

'Well,' said Tom.

Justine chewed her lip for a second or two, then made a decision. 'Then I'd love to come. I usually go to church with the whole family for Christmas, but this year everything has been a bit different and my parents are busy with other things.'

'So, you're not seeing them at all over Christmas?'

Justine hesitated as a brief feeling of nostalgia stole over her and again the sense of loneliness that she'd experienced on the first day. What would it be like, she wondered, to sit down for Christmas lunch without Janos to clown around over the jokes from the crackers, without Uncle Jethro toasting Christmas over and over in his booming voice? And no Sara to fight with over the last mince pie? Something pressed behind her eyes, but she hid it with a shrug. 'No, but don't worry. I'm getting used to things being different, and I'm not sentimental about it.'

Liar.

'Great,' said Tom, although he didn't appear convinced. 'Meet me in the courtyard outside the café, and we'll drive down. Richard doesn't walk so well these days.'

'Well, well,' said Dawn after Tom had left to get changed for the party. 'Looks like you have a date.'

'Hardly. It's only church.'

'If you say so.' Almost but not quite hiding a knowing smile, Dawn shrugged. 'Right, let's get these trays brought in. You're okay doing it on your own? I'll start getting the smoked salmon ready.'

Justine took a couple of trays and left the kitchen. She passed Tom's office at the end of the flag-stoned corridor, the door still open but the room in darkness, apart from the colour-changing Christmas tree, now that he'd finished for the day. The entrance to the living areas was through a door with studs and green baize on the other side, and Justine found the small ante-room off the large, formal drawing room easily enough as it was situated just past the main hall where anyone — in the olden days, full-time servants — had access to both dining and the drawing room adjacent to it without being seen.

She pushed open the double glass door to the ante-room, admiring the engravings depicting birds wading in a stream — storks or cranes, she didn't know. They were beautiful and seemed familiar, but she couldn't remember where she'd seen doors like that before.

A low hum rose from the drawing room where the guests, who'd arrived early, were assembled, and two teenagers clad in white and black waited for her next to the food tables. One of them was clearly Dawn's daughter judging by the hazel eyes and light brown hair so like her mother's. Bottles of champagne were already arranged on another table covered with a thick white cloth, as well as rows upon rows of champagne flutes waiting to be filled.

How many guests had Priscilla invited? The whole village, and then some, by the look of it.

The two girls giggled when they saw Justine. 'Do you know how to open a bottle of fizz?' asked the one who must be Dawn's daughter.

'Sure. Let me show you.' Justine put down the trays and grabbed a bottle and a cloth napkin from a pile left there for the purposes of wiping the neck of the bottle after topping up a glass.

You had to hand it to Priscilla; she knew how to do things right.

'The trick is to twist the bottle, not the cork,' Justine explained and held onto the top with a firm grip while she turned the bottle in her other hand. The cork came away with a muted pop and a fine mist of carbon dioxide.

'There,' she said. 'Easy-peasy. Now you give it a go.'

'Thanks.'

The girls both opened a bottle each without mishap and Justine returned to the kitchen to collect the rest of the trays of savouries. When she brought in the last tray of smoked salmon and homemade blinis, the party was in full swing, and the low hum from earlier had become a loud hubbub of voices.

It hadn't originally bothered her not being invited, but now that it sounded like everyone was having a fantastic time, envy suddenly got the better of her. She stuck her head around the door of the richly decorated room to see if she could sneak in unnoticed and sample a glass of champagne and some of the canapes she and Dawn had so painstakingly assembled, but it was not to be.

Priscilla must have had a sixth sense

as just as that moment she chose to look in the direction of the door and caught Justine's eyes with a haughty lift of her eyebrows, and Justine quickly ducked out of the way again.

Damn.

She laughed to herself. Poor Priscilla. She was so determined to shut Justine out — God only knew why — that it was tempting to do something to provoke her, just for the fun of it. She decided against it though as she couldn't be bothered with the resulting fall-out.

And, besides, Dawn hadn't been invited either so Justine wasn't the only one.

Instead, to kill time before meeting up with Tom, whom she'd spotted deep in conversation with a group of men, farmers if their fresh complexion like Tom's was anything to go by, she decided to have a little wander.

The only time she'd been anywhere near this part of the house was on the first day when Tom had taken her to meet Henry and his family in the small sitting room on the other side of the great hall, a less grand room than the drawing room and dining room where the party was being held.

The great hall looked like a giant chessboard with its white and black marbled floor, and the walls were painted a delicate duck egg blue. A large painting of a woman in a Victorian cinched-waist dress hung above the marble mantelpiece — an ancestor most likely — and a carpeted staircase with gleaming mahogany banisters led to the first and second floors, lined with other portraits.

Holly, this time real, had been tied around the handrail with a wide, red ribbon, and whilst it was pretty, it was also impractical for anyone wishing to hold on when going upstairs.

On impulse she started up the stairs, her footfall cushioned by the thick carpet, studying the portraits as she went.

The first was of a man in fusilier's

uniform, again Victorian which Justine could see from his magnificent sideburns. Maybe the first baronet and husband of the woman above the mantelpiece. Other portraits followed. She didn't know much about art history, but she knew about costumes, and she could tell that the paintings became more and more recent as she went further up.

Her eyes widened as she stopped in front of a portrait of a man the spitting image of Henry. Except it wasn't Henry because the sitter's clothes belonged to an era a few decades back. It was his grandfather, Lord Brooks, whom she'd met by Rexus's cage. Obviously he was a lot older now but still recognisably the man in the painting. She'd heard Tom intermittently referring to him as Richard and the Old Man. Did he mind the nickname, she wondered?

She smiled. It was amazing how Henry looked so much like his grandfather had in his youth. There could be no doubt about his heritage.

The woman in the portrait next to

Henry's grandfather looked straight out of *Vogue*. Standing slightly sideways in an open doorway, she wore a white dress with a long full skirt embroidered with black flowers at the hem, which cascaded from a tight bodice. Shorter at the front, the dress invited a cheeky foot in a black pump to poke out from under it, and the posture gave the illusion of a model balancing on the doorstep between one room and the next.

And her face . . .

'What are you doing here?' Priscilla's cut-glass intonation sliced through Justine's daydream.

'I was just looking at the family portraits. I hope that's okay.'

'No, it's not okay,' Priscilla hissed. 'This is *our* home and you can't just go sneaking about as you want. This part of the house is private. You have no business here.'

Something in Justine snapped. Perhaps it was the combination of the recent changes to her life, the creeping loneliness, the sense of being on the outside, as well as her slight worry about Rexus and her bigger worry about the future. Perhaps it was the unsettling feelings she was developing for Tom, against her better judgment because of course that could go exactly nowhere. But this woman was going to get a piece of her mind.

'You know what? I've just about had enough of you. I'm not some flipping servant, and this isn't *Downton Abbey*. I was invited here by Henry's grandfather to look after the lion for a while and instead I find myself skivvying for nothing and babysitting two spoiled brats.'

'I. Beg. Your. Pardon?' Priscilla went white and the coldness in her voice could have plunged hell itself into the Ice Age. 'How dare — '

'Actually I do dare. You're no more than me, for all your fine furniture and fancy parties. So, why don't you just shut your face? You'd be doing everyone a bleeding favour!'

Fuming, she pushed past the stunned Priscilla and stomped down the stairs and back to the kitchen. Or gob-smacked might be a better word; she was willing to bet no one had ever spoken to Priscilla like that before.

Well, about time. The cow.

Okay, so she'd gone up the stairs without permission but she hadn't meant any harm. She was only looking at the portraits, not stealing them, for Pete's sake. Priscilla should be proud that someone actually took a genuine interest in the family's history, despite its complexity.

Dawn had finished arranging *petits fours*, and Justine snatched a chocolate and toffee mousse and stuffed it in her mouth.

'Like that, is it? I guess you ran into Lady Muck.'

'She caught me looking at the family portraits on the stairwell. Said I was intruding on the family's privacy.'

'Really? That's odd. She's usually eagerness itself to show off the ancestors — Henry's, not hers — to anyone who can be bothered listening to her.'

Justine shrugged. 'Well, I've come to the conclusion that she simply doesn't like me.'

'You are awfully pretty, maybe that's why. But it's still odd.' Dawn took a platter in each hand and balanced one on her arm. 'Don't worry about these ones. I'll bring them in myself. Quite keen to see how my daughter is getting on. Don't be late for your date.'

'It's not a date!' Justine called after her, then went back to her room to fetch her jacket, hat and gloves. It had been bright and sunny all day, but clouds had blown in and the temperature had dropped drastically since it went dark.

Perhaps it might snow on Christmas Day. She hoped so.

7

Justine found Tom where he'd said he'd be, outside the café. He'd ditched the Barbour jacket for a navy blue pea coat and had tamed his red hair with an elastic band. The coat suited him.

'I've already driven Richard to the church,' he said. 'He's on the parish council and wanted to get there early, but I suspect it was just an excuse to escape Priscilla's party.'

'It sounded lively,' said Justine.

'It was, but it's never been his cup of tea. Losing both his sons before their time has made him rather impatient when it comes to chit-chat and social niceties, I'm afraid. Come, let's walk.'

'Where's your car?'

'I left it there and walked back to meet you. We literally only stayed at the party for half an hour, so I had time. It's not far anyway.'

They followed the lane leading from the house down to the main road and headed towards the village. Although not yet seven o'clock, it was nearly pitch black. Justine had grown up with the bright lights of the arena, and when those lights were extinguished and she wasn't performing, the back lot itself had never been completely dark because of the proximity of the other caravans.

A darkened country lane was a different kettle of fish, and for a moment her imagination got the better of her, conjuring up images of strange beasts and people with murderous intent. Instinctively she drew a little closer to Tom.

He took her hand as the most natural thing in the world, as if he'd sensed her unease.

Pull away, her head demanded but she found that she couldn't. Instead she gave herself over to the sensation of the warmth of his hand even through her woollen gloves, and the way he seemed to radiate strength and protection.

Which was totally fanciful, what with

her guarding her independence so fiercely; she'd never felt the need for anyone's protection, and didn't need it now either on this deserted road.

Yeah, right.

The realisation that she was fooling herself warmed her inside and out. Would it really be so difficult to be with Tom even if he wasn't of the circus?

The moon peeped out from behind a cloud, and the lane was suddenly bathed in light. Tom stopped, and facing her, he took her other hand.

'It's a shame we don't have snow. It would've been very . . . picturesque.'

'Or romantic,' said Justine and nearly kicked herself.

Tom grinned, an almost wolfish grimace in the cool, white light. 'That was the word I wanted to use but I didn't want you to think I was setting the stage for something. I just wanted to be with you, alone, for a little while.'

Justine swallowed hard. 'I wasn't thinking that at all.'

He put his arm around her and

pulled her close.

'Tom . . . ' she said, uncertain of whether to pull away or not.

'I know,' he whispered. His warm hands slid around the back of her neck, and gently he tilted her head up for a kiss.

Desire rammed into her when their lips met, with such force she gasped. She'd been kissed before, of course she had, and had had a few boyfriends too, but in the circus people came and went, and she'd never been enough attached to anyone to let it disrupt her routine.

This was different. She clung to Tom as if they were two jigsaw pieces that had finally been put together.

But reality had a way of creeping in when it was least wanted.

'Oh, Tom,' she whispered when they came up for air. 'This can never work. I spend eight months of the year on the road, and . . . and you're here, with your family where you belong. Henry needs you, and I've seen you with the girls. They adore you, and you're so patient with them.'

'So that's a no, then?' He gave a little smile tinged with both cheekiness and sadness and brushed back a strand of her hair which had escaped from her beanie hat.

'It's probably for the best. Don't you think?'

'I'm a patient man.'

Justine shrugged in her coat and changed the subject. 'Aren't we going to be late?'

'Shit, yes! Here, take my hand, and we'll run for it.' He grabbed her hand again and started pulling her along with him.

'I can run on my own,' she protested.

'I know but it's more fun together.'

Laughing, she allowed him to lead the way just as the moon disappeared behind a cloud again and left them in total darkness.

What a shame it hadn't snowed. It would have been straight out of a Hollywood film to kiss in the snow, even if things couldn't go anywhere between them.

* * *

They arrived at the village church just as the bells had finished pealing for the Christmas service. The space was packed more heavily than Justine had imagined it would be for such a small village, but people clearly came from further afield for this particular service.

Like herself.

Tom indicated a pew towards the back where there was some room and signalled for Justine to slide in first. As she did so, an elderly man moved his hat and scarf from the space beside him to make room for them, and she realised Lord Brooks had kindly kept a place for them.

'Good evening, we meet again,' he whispered, although loudly as those who are a little hard of hearing often do. 'I didn't introduce myself properly last time. I'm Richard, Henry's grandfather, which you've probably worked out, and Tom's too when he lets me.'

Tom grinned. 'He's not really, but you know that.'

'So, is the lion letting you have the evening off? As I said before, he's a magnificent beast.'

Frowning, Tom looked from one to the other. 'You've met? I wasn't aware of that.'

'Only the one time,' Lord Brooks replied, staring intently at Justine. 'I go and see the lion in the evenings, when everyone else is safely tucked up in their beds. Reckon he appreciates my company. On one occasion this young lady and I bumped into each other.' He turned a sharp eye on Tom. 'And don't you go telling me not to be up late and nonsense like that, like my grandson's bossy wife!'

Tom set his lips in a firm line as if he was trying not to smile. 'Wouldn't dream of it.'

'Shh!' A stern-looking lady in the pew in front of them turned and glared.

'Oh, keep your blue rinse on, you silly old fool,' said Richard. Justine barely suppressed a snigger.

'Really!' The woman sent them a furious look and turned away again with a huff.

'I think that's us told,' Tom murmured, his eyes shining with mischief like Richard's. Justine felt her good mood almost bubbling over. Despite not seeing her parents, and despite that earlier altercation with Priscilla, Christmas promised to be entertaining.

'Pah! God gave us the ability to converse for a reason,' Richard muttered. Nevertheless he lowered his tone and patted Justine's hand. 'We have a lot to discuss, you and I, but now is not the time.'

To the satisfaction of the woman in the pew in front of them, Richard gave himself over to the service with devotion. At some point Justine thought he might have had tears in his eyes, which took her by surprise. Maybe it shouldn't have, she reflected. The old man had suffered the most terrible loss imaginable, the death of not only one but both his sons, and may have turned to religion with extra fervour.

But it was Christmas, and it was hard to suppress the excited energy that flowed through the congregation, putting a smile on the faces of both adults and children. And the choir, who must be in to amateur dramatics, made the children laugh with their interpretation of the nativity scene, complete with braying sheep and clucking hens.

'Oh dear Lord, please make them stop!' Richard muttered to himself, and Tom grinned.

The air was fragrant with the scent of pine, dried oranges, and cloves from the potpourri decorations at the end of each pew, and the smell of something warm and spicy wafted in from the adjoining church hall. Justine's own Christmas cheer began to build further, and she leaned back in her seat and joined in with the carols. Priscilla could keep her expensive champagne.

After the service everyone gathered in the church hall for mince pies and mulled wine. As Tom went to fetch the three of them a glass and a pie, Richard introduced Justine to some of his acquaintances, who were all fascinated when they learned who she was, then he left her to circulate the room.

'A lion?' said one woman, clutching the stem of her glass in a gloved hand. 'But isn't that dangerous?'

'Everything is dangerous if you don't know how to handle it,' Justine replied. 'Like cars, for instance.'

The woman nodded. 'I suppose so. I've never thought of it like that.'

'It's very exciting having an animal like that in the village,' said a man with a tartan cap in his coat pocket and a strong Norfolk burr. He turned out to be the local historian, and it didn't take him long to get on to what appeared to be a favourite subject of his, that of Stonybrook's history. 'I believe Lord Brooks has a few other animals. Is he planning on opening a zoo? There used to be one, many years ago. A menagerie, they called it.'

'I don't think he is,' said Justine, 'but maybe it isn't a bad idea. There are lots of animals, of all kinds, in animal rescue centres, which may otherwise have to be put down. I've also noticed an aviary in the grounds, although it's very neglected.'

'Nothing a lick of paint can't cure,' said the historian.

Justine had her doubts. That aviary would need more than a lick of paint, and the upkeep of maintaining a populated birdcage would probably cost more than she thought the estate could cope with. But she didn't say that; instead she smiled and made her way over to Tom who was holding out a glass to her.

She lifted her glass to Tom's. 'Cheers.'

'And to you.'

Their eyes met, Tom's full of longing, and her own . . . well, she could hardly see herself but she hoped he couldn't read her as well as she could read him. If so, he would see her confusion.

'Some people have suggested a zoo on the estate,' she said, to divert his thoughts. 'Like the one Stonybrook had in late Victorian times.'

'Yes, I knew about that,' said Tom. 'They closed it down at the outbreak of the First World War because there was no one left to manage it. Back then they didn't have female zookeepers like we do today.' He winked.

'Thankfully times have changed,' Justine replied tartly.

'I was only teasing. I'm sure you can do anything you set your mind to.'

'Really?' Justine scrutinised his face for signs of sarcasm but found only frankness. 'That's about the nicest thing anyone has ever said to me.'

'You deserve people saying nice things to you. For the rest of your life.' Tom held her eyes again, and heat rose in her cheeks.

'The thing is, Tom — '

'So, what's this business about a zoo?' Richard had returned and now slid his arm through Justine's for support. 'Oates over there tells me you're planning to open one at Stonybrook.'

Justine laughed. 'If he said that, then he's jumping to conclusions. He mentioned that there used to be one, and I said it wasn't such a bad idea.'

Richard squeezed her arm. 'I would like to commission you to set up a new one. We need more than a porcupine and a couple of hyenas to keep the beast company.'

Her jaw dropped. 'But the cost . . . ?'

'Tosh. I'm releasing the funds. I've decided that we should reinstate the former menagerie. That's what I want at Stonybrook, and I want people to come from far and wide to visit us.'

'Are you sure, Richard?' asked Tom. 'There are a few other matters at the estate which perhaps require priority. Like a new roof over the east wing.'

'I'm releasing funds for that too. Please inform Henry for me.'

'Of course, but — '

'And now I'd like for you to drive me

home. I tire easily these days,' he added for Justine's benefit.

'Naturally,' Tom replied. 'Justine?'

'I'm ready.'

While Tom fetched their coats, which they'd hung in the vestibule when they came in, Justine guided Richard around the room so he could say his goodbyes.

'I knew your mother,' he suddenly said to her. 'She was very beautiful.'

'She still is. I guess I don't really think much about it because she's my mother, but yes she is. But, how do you know her?'

The old man sighed, his former mischievous look replaced by sudden sadness, and the pause gave Justine the impression that he was about to tell her something important. Then he squared his shoulders, and she thought she must have misread him.

'Well, Circus Belmont came to town many years ago, and they hired the south paddock to pitch the tent. They did several performances which were well attended.'

'I don't remember but my uncle told me about it once. Strangely we've never toured in East Anglia since. I always thought it was because of audience numbers but clearly not.'

Tom returned with their coats and Justine's jacket, and helped Richard put on his, then led them to the car park. As the Richard climbed in, Tom muttered to himself.

'A zoo? What next? A blimmin' circus?'

'I heard that, my friend,' came the gruff reply from inside the Jeep. 'All in good time. All in good time.'

Tom rolled his eyes. 'Heaven help us.'

* * *

When they got back to Stonybrook, Tom parked outside the main entrance and helped Richard up to his suite of rooms on the second floor.

Priscilla's party was still going on, although quieter now that many of the guests had left, but he had no desire to join them. The stragglers would be Priscilla's sister and brother and their families who were staying for Christmas. He liked them well enough, but Richard's words about releasing funds had him worried, and he was in no mood for partying.

Was the old guy losing it?

He returned to the Jeep hoping that Justine was waiting for him, but understandably she'd left, so he drove around to the yard and knocked on the door to her apartment.

'I'd have driven you to your door if you'd waited,' he said when she answered. 'You must think me a poor excuse for a gentleman.'

She was already dressed for bed in a pair of pyjama bottoms and a T-shirt even though it was only just nine, and rubbed her arms against the cold. Tom wanted to pull her close and warm her under his coat but knew this would mean crossing way too many boundaries, so he managed to resist.

'It's okay,' she said. 'I figured Richard

needed some help with the stairs.'

'He did. Henry has offered to swap rooms, but Richard insists on staying on the top floor. He's a stubborn old fool if you ask me.'

Justine smiled. 'He does give the impression of being very set in his ways.'

'That's the polite way of putting it,' Tom snorted. 'Anyway, it's cold, and you shouldn't be out here, but since you're not doing anything tomorrow, I wondered if you fancied going riding before my attendance is required at Christmas dinner. I *did* promise.'

'That'd be lovely.'

'Till tomorrow, then. Eleven o'clock okay?'

'Perfect. Can I have Coco, please?' she added with a sideways smile.

'I was about to suggest that. Coco seemed fine with you, and Homer is used to me.'

They said goodnight, almost formally as if that kiss on the way to church had never happened, and Tom went to his own rooms wishing that he'd at least given her a peck on the cheek.

What must she think of him, grabbing her like that and then . . . nothing? That he was playing with her, no doubt.

For the first time he cursed himself for not having tried to date a little bit after splitting up with his wife. Then he might have been more knowledgeable about the whole dating game and not acted like such a moron.

* * *

When she'd said good night to Tom, Justine stood for a moment leaning against the closed door, her heart beating wildly. She'd been so close to inviting him in and asking him to stay the night, but had stopped herself just in time.

He'd seemed genuine enough when he'd kissed her, and they'd had a really nice time together at the church with Lord Brooks. The sense of comfort she experienced in his company was the kind you felt around someone you'd known a long time.

Maybe they had. Maybe it was destiny, and they'd been waiting for each other across an eternity, like the hero and heroine in a novel.

Or maybe she needed to have her head examined.

Resolutely she pushed away from the door and went into the bathroom to get ready for bed. When she unzipped her washbag, a large spider jumped out and ran up her arm.

'Ugh!' With a squeak she shook it off, and it landed in the bathtub where it sat motionless like a giant, hairy freckle on the pristine porcelain.

With a mixture of revulsion and fascination she stared it at, but when it looked as if it wasn't going anywhere straight away, she went to fetch a large drinking glass in the kitchen and tore off a strip of board from a cereal packet. Then she coaxed the spider inside the glass, put on her jacket and carried the glass downstairs to the storage room. She let the spider out next to the big deep freezer and watched it scuttle underneath and out of sight.

It was odd, though. Out of habit she always zipped up her washbag when she'd finished using her toiletries, because she was so used to keeping her personal things contained in the cramped caravan.

So how could a spider of that size get inside?

8

The task of passing on the message from the old man to Henry turned out to be as tricky as Tom had envisaged. Not Henry, although he grumbled about the wisdom of it and Tom could hardly blame him as the purpose of releasing the funds seemed frivolous in the extreme.

No, it was Priscilla as usual who made her displeasure known. Loudly.

He'd sought out Henry in his office before breakfast in the hope of finding him alone, but contrary to her usual morning routine Priscilla was up early and was poring over the figures with him, an unusual thing for them to be doing Christmas morning. Perhaps the finances were in a worse state than the old man thought.

Tom took a deep breath and relayed the message as gently as he could. Even so, Priscilla still hit the roof.

'What? The *aviary*? Oh, my goodness, what *is* the old fool thinking?'

'Darling — ' Henry began.

'Don't you 'darling' me! I don't know what the matter with your grandfather is, but he must be going senile. You have to stop him!'

'I can't, and you know that. The estate is not entailed, Grandpa isn't dead yet — not that I want him to go any time soon — and he can do what he likes and will the whole boiling lot to whoever he pleases. Even an animal charity if he chooses to. You know that.'

'But . . . but that's insane!' Priscilla began pacing up and down in her stilettos. '*He* is insane!' Furiously she turned to Tom. 'And why you? Why can't *he* tell us?'

Tom shrugged, having thought as much himself. But then again the old man had probably wanted to avoid just such a scene as this one. Not so much of a fool after all.

Priscilla paced some more, wringing her hands. 'I bet it's to do with that girl.

That . . . that circus princess!'

'What can she possible have to do with it?' asked Tom.

'Oh, you wouldn't understand. Of course she has something to do with it! She's probably twisted Henry's grandfather around her little finger. He's always been fascinated by the circus and circus life. *And* she goes to church! Did you know she was awfully rude to me yesterday? And in my own home.'

'No, I didn't know that, but I suspect you probably deserved it.'

Turning puce, Priscilla opened and closed her mouth, guppy-like, to say something but her indignation was so strong she couldn't get a word out.

'Now, now, Tom,' said Henry mildly, 'no need for that.' To his wife he said, 'I dare say we shall survive.'

'Survive?' Priscilla found her voice again. '*Survive*? I want more from life that just surviving. Your inheritance will be spent before you even get it!'

'It's *not* my inheritance. The majority of it belongs to the manor. How many times do I have to tell you?' Henry rubbed his hands across his eyes. 'To be honest with you, I've never imagined myself as a baronet, or running an estate, but I can't do anything about the title. That will always be mine whether I want it or not. No, I always pictured you and me and the kids living at the home farm when the tenants go. That's the kind of life I would prefer.'

'The home farm?' Priscilla spat.

'Well, what's so wrong with that? I know it needs work, but it's part of the estate, and I'm sure I could persuade Grandfather to set some money aside so we can bring it into the twenty-first century. The outbuildings are perfect for holiday lets, and the garden is big enough so we could have a swimming pool. We'd have a good life. I could go back to being an accountant, and you could manage the rentals. We could see more of the world, and not have this burden of responsibility hanging over us. I don't even want Stonybrook.'

'But I do!' his wife shouted. 'You

need to have your grandfather declared mentally incompetent, get a power of attorney or something. He's a lunatic!'

'Mummy? Daddy?' Portia had appeared in the doorway behind Tom, in her nightie, clutching a soft toy in one hand and rubbing the sleep from her eyes with the other. 'Why are you shouting?'

Ignoring his daughter and clenching his fists, Henry rose from his desk chair. 'I will do no such thing, and you will not speak about my grandfather like that. Do you hear?'

His normally mild manner gone, Henry rose to his full height of six feet, and Priscilla for all her bluster and stilettos suddenly seemed smaller. Shocked even.

'Please, Daddy, don't shout at Mummy like that!'

Their eyes locked on each other, her parents didn't seem to have noticed her, not even when Portia, her eyes brimming with tears, tugged at her father's sleeve. Tom's heart went out to her, and in the ensuing silence, heavy with resentment and fermenting anger, he shifted towards the door. Witnessing someone else's family argument wasn't how he'd planned on spending Christmas Day, but just as he was about to slip out, he remembered something he wanted to ask Priscilla.

'I know it's probably the wrong time to ask a favour, but I'm taking Justine riding this morning and wondered if she could borrow your riding helmet and boots? I doubt she brought things like that with her.'

He braced himself for another outburst from his cousin's wife, but Priscilla slowly turned her head in his direction, almost zombie-like with a curious glazed look in her eyes as if she was about to cry.

'Riding? Sure, take what you need. I don't suppose it matters now.'

Tom thanked her and made his escape. He'd seen Priscilla angry before but not Henry, and he began to wonder if there wasn't more to his cousin than met the eye, something other than the hen-pecked husband.

He hoped so. Priscilla went too far sometimes.

* * *

It had snowed in the night, not a lot, but enough to cover the yard and the fields with a fine dusting. Although the sun was out, the air was crisp and bit into Tom's cheeks as he went to the stables.

He'd spent the morning in his office wrapping and re-wrapping a present for Justine, using up most of a roll of paper in his butter-fingered attempt at making the parcel look presentable, and the last person he expected to run into when he went to the stables was Priscilla.

'Oh,' he said, taken aback. 'Everything all right?'

'Just looking for Portia,' she replied, her cheeks flushed. 'She insisted on giving the horses a carrot.'

'Did you find her?'

Priscilla's eyes slid sideways. 'No. She must've left. I think she's trying to avoid me.'

I wonder why, thought Tom.

'Are you sure you're looking after these horses properly?' Priscilla demanded. 'They seem a bit neglected.'

'Don't let them fool you. I can assure you they're not.'

'Well, if you say so. By the way, I've left riding boots and helmet in the stable. Lunch is at one. See you then.' She dug her hands inside the pockets of her padded gilet and left.

Justine peeked her head around the corner of the building, grinning, just as Tom was about to step inside.

'I thought she'd never leave,' she said.

'You were wise to hide. She's not in the best of moods today.' Tom handed her the badly wrapped parcel, and she sent him a wry smile when she saw the result of his efforts.

'You didn't have to buy me a present,' she said. 'I'm afraid I haven't bought you anything.' Her cheeks coloured lightly, and she lowered her head to unwrap it.

'It's nothing much.' Tom shifted from one foot to another. 'Just something I had lying around and thought you might like. And since you weren't seeing your family . . . Anyway, Merry Christmas.'

With his hands deep in his pockets he watched her opening the present and delighted in the changing expressions on her face, from intrigue to puzzlement to wonder.

'This is lovely,' she whispered and held up the embroidered bedspread. The material was black cotton and featured two applique lions in traditional African stitching. Tom had brought it back home from Africa years ago.

'I know the flat above the stables quite well, and although it's neat and comfortable, it's not very personal. This, at least, will remind you of where Rexus originally came from even if he was born in captivity. I'm hoping it'll remind you of Stonybrook when you're no longer here.'

And of me, he thought.

'But I couldn't possibly accept this,' she said, her face still a picture of astonishment.

'Of course you can. I want you to have it. I suspect it'll mean more to you than it does to me, and it doesn't fit my bed anyway, so it just sort of hangs over the back of my sofa where you can't really see it.'

'Well, if you're sure . . . '

'I am. Now, let's go riding.'

* * *

'So, when's lunch?' Justine asked as they steered the horses down the country lane. Priscilla's riding helmet turned out to fit her perfectly although the riding boots were a couple of sizes too big. 'Not that I'm angling for an invitation, just curious.'

'One o'clock and it'll be on the dot if I know Priscilla right. She's very organised.' Tom's face clouded over at the memory of that unpleasant scene earlier. Priscilla hadn't looked in the mood for anything other than smashing crockery.

'She certainly is,' Justine replied.

'It's usually jolly enough.' Tom shrugged, to himself more than anything. 'Her brother and sister are here with their families, and they have young children so . . . ' He tailed off, realising she must be missing her own family.

'I'll be okay,' she said as if she'd read his mind. 'Dawn has prepared a plate for me, and this afternoon I'm planning on practising some new acts. Now, is there anywhere we can go so the horses can really stretch their legs? This pace is a little too slow for me.'

'Yep. This way.'

Tom turned off the road and unlocked the gate to a large paddock. 'We lease this land to a farmer, and he leaves his heifers to graze here but still allows me to use it for riding in winter when the animals are indoors. We can let the horses stretch out here.'

'Great.'

Before Tom could reply Justine nudged Coco in the sides and set off in full gallop across the field, laughing as she went and with her blonde hair streaming out from beneath the rim of the helmet.

Enjoyment soared in Tom's chest at her total recklessness, and he spurred Homer to follow, but Justine and Coco had had a head start, and the older horse couldn't keep up.

It didn't matter. As she turned in the saddle and grinned triumphantly back at him it all fell into place.

He was in love. Totally and utterly smitten. Besotted and bamboozled in equal measure. Warm inside from the mere thought of her.

'You're incredible!' he called after her. 'And nuts!'

She didn't hear. Everything happened so fast; first she was in the saddle, elegant and splendid in her wild abandon, then a crumpled heap on the ground.

The air stilled. Tom's heart stopped for one long moment, then beat furiously again as he shouted something intelligible to his own ears which was drowned out by Homer's thunderous hooves. He pulled hard at Homer's reins to stop riding over Justine's prone body.

'No!' In a flash he was beside her, desperately trying to recall what he'd learned on his first aid course years ago. A million thoughts raced through his brain but somehow he managed to collect himself.

Presence of danger.

Homer stood quietly nearby, and Coco was at the end of the paddock with her saddle dangling down one side.

Check.

Response.

He tapped Justine's collarbone gently, and his heart leapt when she moaned quietly.

Check.

Airway. Normal breathing?

Yes, she was breathing. But how badly injured was she? Tom could see no bleeding. Neck? Spine?

When she opened her eyes and sent him a pained smile, Tom nearly wept.

'Are you hurt? And where? Tell me!'

Justine paused for what seemed like ages as she tried to steady her breathing. 'I don't think I am,' she said at last. 'Please help me sit up.'

'Is that wise?' Tom took her hand and placed his arm behind her back for support. 'If your neck . . . '

'No broken bones,' she said with confidence. 'I'm battered and bruised, yes, but I haven't broken anything. I'd be able to tell if I had.' She smiled, less pained now. 'I've broken a few bones in my time so I think I know the signs. Comes with the territory, I'm afraid.'

Tom helped her sit up fully. 'I don't understand. That fall you took, at full gallop, it could have killed you. It would have killed anyone else I suspect. It looked . . . nasty.' He touched her hands, her arms, her head to reassure himself that she really wasn't hurt. And to just feel her, her warmth, the life in her which could so easily have been snuffed out.

'I'm all right. Really.' She let him pull her to her feet, then gently pushed his hands away. 'I know how to fall properly. Learned that from when I was this high.'

She held out her hand to indicate just how high, then suddenly wobbled, and Tom caught her in his arms. This time he didn't let her push him away, but drew her close and whispered in her ear.

'I thought I'd lost you.'

'As I said, I know how to fa — '

He silenced her with his mouth, kissing her hard and almost crushing her soft lips. Kissing him back with the same fervour, she moulded herself to his body, her heart hammering against his chest. Perhaps she was more shaken than she wanted to admit, or maybe, just maybe, she returned his feelings. He was beginning to hope when she extricated herself.

'Stay at Stonybrook,' he whispered. 'Run the menagerie as Richard wants. Stay with *me*.'

'I can't, Tom. My father was right when he said it was time I went my own way. Yes, I love it here at Stonybrook. It's peaceful, and there's a wonderful sense of space, like something I've never experienced before. But I also like to have people around me, lots of people. It's how I grew up. Being around animals and performing is in my blood. I must find another circus.'

'I'll come with you,' he said.

'And do what? Be a hanger-on? There isn't room for hangers-on in the circus, and anyway that kind of life isn't for you. You were made for the type of outdoorsy lifestyle you have here, where you have your horses and your routine. And your almost-grandfather. You love it here. Leaving would tear you apart.'

Looking deep into her sea green eyes, Tom swallowed hard. How could she read him so well? He loved Stonybrook with a passion, and would gladly spend the rest of his days here even after Richard was gone and whatever Henry then chose to do with his life.

He loved the muddy fields, the evergreen woods, the sunrise over the flat, fertile land, the bracing air which put a rosy glow on everyone's cheeks. Here his roots were deeper than they'd ever been anywhere else, even in Africa.

If only Justine felt the same way, but her heart was with the bright lights, the glamour, and the danger she courted on a daily basis. They were poles apart.

He sighed. 'I think we'd better head back. It's getting cold.'

Clouds had blown in from the east bringing the promise of more snow with them, and although Justine by some miracle wasn't hurt, her lips had taken on a blueish tinge and she was shaking, probably from shock. She needed to be back indoors and get warmed up.

She nodded and, to confirm his line of thought, huddled further into her short jacket.

'Are you okay with sitting on Homer? I'll lead both horses once I've caught Coco.'

Fear flashed across her face briefly, but she nodded again, her mouth set in a determined line. She clearly lived by the mantra of 'get back on the horse'. Literally. A circus girl through and through. The thought filled Tom with both admiration and sadness because their worlds were so different.

Coco was hobbling slightly on one of her hind legs when he caught her, probably from adjusting her stride when Justine had toppled sideways and almost in between the horse's legs. The mare had always had a strong instinct for protecting her rider. Gently Tom felt Coco's hock and fetlock but could detect nothing broken. Just a strain then, as he'd hoped, although he did wonder why an accomplished horsewoman like Justine would fall off. Was it perhaps a rabbit hole she didn't see?

Then he inspected the saddle, which had slid sideways. Although Henry and Priscilla didn't ride any more after having sold their own horses, Tom still checked all the harnesses and saddles as a matter of routine. Today he'd tightened the girth as he normally would, and retightened it when Coco had exhaled to prevent the saddle from slipping, but this was commonplace for him and something he did without even thinking about it. By rights the saddle shouldn't have slipped.

He lifted the saddle onto Coco's back again. The horse shied a little and stamped her front legs.

'Easy, easy,' he soothed and reached under her belly for the girth strap.

That was when he noticed it. Still attached to the girth buckles were two of the three billet straps, which held the girth strap to the right side of the saddle. A saddle normally had three billets straps, and two of these would be buckled to the girth strap with the third acting as a spare in case one of the other two broke when out riding. This ensured that the saddle could still be safely used.

Both of the two billet straps in use had detached themselves from under the skirt of the saddle where they were stitched onto the saddle tree.

Tom looked more closely at the stitching, which could occasionally become damaged through water or rot if one wasn't careful. Sure enough, the stitching had been compromised and had snapped. Perhaps water had somehow got in there and damaged it.

But on all three billet straps?

He cursed himself. He was normally so meticulous but had been distracted by Justine's presence in the stables, and he must have overlooked something.

And Justine could have died.

Cold sweat trickled down his spine as he soothed Coco while securing the saddle as best he could. The mare was still a little skittish, and he took her by the reins and led her back to Justine.

She could have *died*.

Leaning against Homer's neck, she looked tired and cold, but determined too, which made him sigh with relief. She made no protest when he helped her up into Homer's saddle, although a barely suppressed groan did escape her. Again, admiration swelled in his chest.

She was quite something.

'I'm going to be black and blue tomorrow,' she said. 'It all comes from having too much fun.'

'You circus folk have a peculiar idea of fun.'

She laughed, then winced. 'Yes, we're a mad lot. If no one's hurt, it's all about getting back up and getting on with it. No rest for the wicked.'

Tom looked up at her, frowning, as he took the reins of both horses and began to walk slowly back. 'Surely you're not planning on practising your wire-walking today? Can't you give yourself some rest for a while?'

'Well yes, I . . . ' She paused as she caught the concern etched on his face which he made no attempt at hiding. 'I suppose I should give myself a break.'

'A couple of days, at least,' said Tom. 'I'd have suggested a week but I doubt you'd listen to me.'

'Probably not.'

'So, you promise?'

'I promise.' Justine leaned forward

and patted Homer on the neck. 'Is he okay with me? You said he doesn't like strangers riding him.'

'He'll be fine with me leading him. He's not going to throw you if that's what you're worried about.'

She chewed her lip. 'I was, a bit. I've had enough flying for one day.'

Against his will he couldn't stop the laughter from bubbling to the surface. 'You really have the most indomitable spirit.'

'*Indomitable spirit*. I like that,' she said, then winced again. 'And now I'd like to get back.'

'Of course.' Tom picked up his pace but only as fast as he felt Coco could walk with her sprain. Thank heaven neither Justine nor Coco were seriously hurt, but by his reckoning it had been a close call. Justine had indeed gone flying, as she put it herself.

Another thought crept up on him as they walked back, and kept niggling at the back of his mind refusing to budge. He was no expert on saddle making but it had looked to him as if the stitching on the billet straps had been cut with a knife.

9

Justine followed Tom's advice and gave herself a break for a few days. In some ways she was grateful for the imposed rest.

Since arriving at Stonybrook her mind had been in turmoil about the future and whether to pursue her own act and how to go about it. Her feelings for Tom complicated everything, and a part of her was tempted to take Lord Brooks up on the offer of reinstating and running the menagerie.

The other part warred fiercely with the temptation of staying put — the lure of life on the road tugging at her; a lifestyle of daily upheaval for sure, but also challenges and excitement. Everything had been so clear in her mind before arriving; settle Rexus, reluctantly because she'd have preferred not to give him up, and resentfully because she didn't have the funds or equipment to keep him, then go back to circus life.

All that had been shot to pieces when arriving here. Even though she'd explained to Tom the importance of going her own way, it was of less consequence than she'd emphasised, but merely a way of actually trying to persuade herself it was the right thing.

It could be so easy to give in to that temptation. Life at Stonybrook was a total contrast to her life before. It offered comfort and safety, and it was almost as if the place itself begged her to put down roots. The urge came over her every morning she pulled back her curtains and looked out over the misty, tranquil parkland. Despite Priscilla presiding over everyone. It would give her and Tom a chance to develop their relationship — not that they actually had one, not really — and see where it took them.

What held her back was the uncertainty of what would come after, one concern being what would happen if she and Tom couldn't make it work, or if Lord Brooks's menagerie plans turned out to be unrealistic. This time there would be no extended circus family to fall back on as she'd always done before when in doubt about anything.

It was like performing a trapeze act without a safety net.

'And for someone who's used to taking things as they come, you do worry an awful lot,' she muttered to her own mirror image as she was getting dressed, a little slowly because of her bruises.

In the end her rivalling thoughts had driven her outside and down to the edge of the woods to where Tom had created the perfect wire-walking set-up for her. First she said hello to Rexus who seemed a little grumpy, perhaps because Tom had insisted on looking after the lion so Justine could rest.

At least that was what she told herself because in reality Rexus had no real need of her.

Greeting her, the lion rolled on the ground a few times, then turned his back on her and sauntered back to his favourite spot on a large boulder and lay down.

She left him to his nap. When she reached the edge of the woods, she unzipped her jacket, took off her boots and put on her wire-walking shoes, soft lace-up leather slippers with no soles, similar to a gymnastics shoe, before swinging herself up on the wire. Balancing on the wire tightener at the tree end, she tested the tautness of the wire itself before stepping out onto it.

To her chagrin the centre of her balance was a little off, perhaps due to stiffness from her bruises. And she soon worked up a sweat as she forced herself back on the wire whenever she missed her footing. Finally, after a couple of hours of hard graft with her father's words echoing in her head — *practice doesn't make perfect, only perfect practice makes perfect* — she sensed a return to her previous level of fitness and poise, and she punched the air in triumph.

'I wish I could do that.' Cordelia

must have been watching her for some time, but in her concentration Justine had barely registered her surroundings.

'It takes a lot of practice,' she admitted. 'And I'm not as good as I used to be.' The thought struck her the second time in the past few weeks that she'd never actually been that good in the first place, merely mediocre. She'd always put it down to being preoccupied with helping her parents, in particular her father, so that she'd only managed to develop her own act sufficiently to be no more than a pause act, or an assistant to another artist. But maybe the explanation was to do with ability — what if she'd never be better than that? Who'd want to hire her? She could also juggle five balls and ride a monocycle at the same time, which was another pause act, but the wire-walking had never been spectacular.

However, she suspected Cordelia was a little too young to understand feelings she had difficulty making sense of herself.

'Is it because you fell off the horse on Christmas Day? Tom told us.'

'It probably has something to do with that.' Justine kept her answer vague and changed the subject. 'Shouldn't you be with your cousins? I thought they were staying until New Year.'

'Don't want to. Cousin Patrick says that Tibbie is an ugly cat, and the baby poos all the time. It smells really bad.'

Justine pictured the snub-nosed Persian and couldn't help agreeing with Cousin Patrick.

'And Portia won't let me play with the twins,' Cordelia continued with a pout. 'She says they can't be bothered with little girls, but I can't be bothered with them. All they talk about is clothes. Portia doesn't even like clothes, she's just pretending so they'll like her. And they talk about boys. Boys are horrible. Yuck!'

Justine laughed. 'One day you'll like boys too, trust me. Not all of them are horrible.'

A particular red-haired man appeared

before her inner eyes, and she looked away so Cordelia couldn't see the sudden heat in her face. Over the last two days he'd been knocking on her door at regular intervals to make sure she was all right, had brought her painkillers and even some provisions so she could cook for herself in the flat, although Dawn had made sure there was plenty she could help herself to in the estate kitchen before she went off on her Christmas break. It turned out that it was Tom who had stocked up her fridge in the first place before she arrived.

In the end she'd had to insist quietly that she was fine and just needed some peace, but this was far from the truth. Several times she'd been close to inviting him in, but it was the thought of what would happen afterwards that had held her back.

Too many complications.

'No, thank you,' said Cordelia so stiffly that Justine laughed so hard she nearly lost her balance again and had to wobble back to the tree for support.

'Can you teach me?' the girl asked suddenly.

'Teach you? I . . . ' Justine thought for a moment. 'Yes, I suppose I could.' She climbed down from the tree and tried not to think about the expression of hurt on Tom's face when she'd fired off that last comment about needing peace. What was she to do about him?

Holding out her hand to Cordelia, she said, 'Come and I'll show you what to do.'

She helped Cordelia up the tree and told her to hold on to her arm. The wire was only three feet off the ground and it was easy enough for her to stretch her arm up so Cordelia could hold onto it as a near-vertical support.

'It's a little difficult in winter boots,' she explained, 'but at least you won't cut your feet on the wire.'

Cordelia clung to her outstretched arm. 'Does it hurt your feet?'

'Not any more. I've learned how to grip the wire with my toes, and if I slide my foot forward carefully, it's usually fine. But in the beginning I used to cut myself all the time, even with my special shoes on.'

'But I won't, will I?'

'No, you'll be fine,' Justine reassured her. 'So, now that you're holding on to my arm, do you think you could move forward on the wire a little bit? It's okay, I've got you,' she added, when Cordelia hesitated. That was the tricky part about learning to wire-walk; when you were on the ground, three feet seemed like nothing, but when you were up on the wire and about to take your first step, the drop suddenly felt like the Grand Canyon.

'Just imagine you're stepping out on a plank of wood or a fallen tree trunk. I noticed a big tree trunk in the woods earlier — I bet you and Portia have walked across that many times and not even worried about it.'

And when your mother isn't watching, she added to herself.

Cordelia nodded. 'I like playing on it, but Portia says it's boring and for babies. And sometimes I climb the trees in the park. I'm better than her and can get much higher.'

'I bet you can,' Justine replied. 'Now, let's see if we can't teach you a trick or two which you can show off to Portia. Then she might stop calling you a baby.'

She guided Cordelia out onto the wire while allowing the child to use her arm for support. Cordelia wobbled at first but soon got the hang of it and, with Justine's arm for support, walked back and forth across the wire several times.

'Again, again!' she squealed with delight and tugged Justine along as she nearly ran across the wire for the third time.

After about an hour, Justine was flushed from the exertion, and her arm was tired from being in the upright position, so she suggested that Cordelia tried without support.

'I don't want to! I'll fall down!'

'No, you won't. I'll be there to make

sure you don't. And if you miss your footing I'll catch you. All right?'

Cordelia hesitated, then nodded with a prim but determined expression on her face. Justine couldn't help smiling; again Cordelia reminded her of her cousin Sara when she persisted with a new act she hadn't quite got the hang of but insisted on doing anyway.

She wondered what Sara was doing now? Her uncle and aunt had gone away for Christmas, and she presumed Sara had gone with them. It was unlikely they'd be back yet. Justine missed her three cousins most of all and decided to give them a call when she thought it possible to get hold of them. She wasn't the only one who'd been affected by the circus closing their doors and had to stop feeling sorry for herself.

Cordelia's first unsupported step onto the wire brought her back to what she was doing, and she followed Cordelia's progress, ready to catch her if she fell. When Cordelia reached the middle of the wire and began to sway precariously, Justine stepped forward and offered her hand.

It was only then she realised she'd been holding her breath. For some reason it had become a matter of pride to her that Cordelia succeeded, more important than her own attempt at regaining her ability.

Perhaps this was what it felt like being a teacher; when your pupils did well, you shared their reward. A warm feeling of achievement spread from the centre of her chest when Cordelia reached the other end of the wire almost unaided.

Maybe other children would be interested in learning the skills she had to share?

She pushed the thought aside. 'Okay, one more time,' she said, 'and this time you do it all yourself.'

'I can't,' protested Cordelia. 'I need to practise more.'

'You practise as you do it. It's the only way.'

'But it's hard!'

'Just because something is hard, doesn't mean we shouldn't try.' Her father's words again. 'I know you can do it.'

Cordelia looked doubtful, then she gritted her teeth and tried again. This time she was near the end when she started to wobble, and she almost tumbled the last few feet to the safety of the cedar tree.

'I did it! I did it!'

'Well done, Dilly.' Behind them Tom was clapping his hands.

At the sight of his smile Justine's concentration went the way of the dodos, and all she could think of was how sexy he looked in jeans and a navy blue Guernsey fisherman's jumper. He'd slung a plain grey woollen scarf around his neck, which complemented his red hair, and held his gloves under his arm while clapping. The applause was for Cordelia, but the smile belonged to Justine.

So, maybe he'd forgiven her for her

comment about needing peace.

Heat flushed in her face, and her heart started racing. That stupid heart which wouldn't do what it was told. It's only Tom, for Pete's sake, she thought. Stop acting like a lovesick teenager.

But there was no denying the effect he had on her every time she saw him.

Damn.

Tom broke the spell as he lifted Cordelia down. 'Aren't you a star?' he said and winked. 'I bet Portia can't do that.'

'But *I* can.' Cordelia smiled smugly. 'And she can't make Rexus count either.'

Tom set Cordelia on the ground. 'The lion can count? I didn't know that. I thought he only performed that trick in the ring.'

'He can. Justine, can we show Tom? Please, please!' Excited, Cordelia started jumping up and down.

'Well, it's getting kind of cold . . . ' Justine began.

'Oh please, oh please!' Cordelia begged again.

Tom looked from one to the other. 'Dilly, if Justine is tired, perhaps we . . . '

Tears welled up in Cordelia's eyes. 'But I wanted you to see!'

'All right,' Justine agreed before Cordelia's tears began flowing in earnest. She could handle a lion, but tears . . .

When she was teaching Cordelia the wire, she'd forgotten to change back into her UGG boots, and only now that she was no longer wrapped up in concentration did she become aware of how cold her feet were in the thin gym shoes. But at least she'd be up on the branch overhanging the enclosure and off the frozen ground. It wouldn't take long, and she could put her boots on afterwards.

'Are you sure?' asked Tom. 'What about your injuries? You can't be over that yet.'

She brushed him off. 'I'm black and blue as I knew I would be but otherwise I'm fine. I'll do it if you and Cordelia promise to stay behind the spectator barrier so Rexus can focus.'

'We will,' said Cordelia.

Justine put on her jacket, which she'd left on the ground when practising, grateful for the sudden warmth. She was colder and stiffer than she'd thought.

By the enclosure she swung herself up in the tree as she'd done last time, satisfied to see that Tom had cut the low hanging branch as she'd asked him to do. Balancing carefully, aware that her muscles were cold and tired, she moved along the branch to the suspended pieces of wood with numbers on. Rexus who'd showed very little interest in her earlier, perked up and placed himself expectantly by the numbers looking up at her and waiting for his cue.

The lion didn't disappoint, and Cordelia and Tom were clapping enthusiastically when Justine joined them again.

'That's impressive,' said Tom. 'I remember Rexus doing it when we first saw you in the circus, and I was impressed back then.'

'It's a trick!' Cordelia shouted triumphantly. 'And I know how to do it, but I'm not telling.'

'Really? You don't say?' Tom winked at Justine. 'I'd never have thought it was a trick.'

Dusk had started to fall as they made their way back to the house. Tom took Justine's hand as any normal couple might, and she let him, enjoying the strength of his grip and the warmth seeping through two sets of gloves.

Cordelia saw them holding hands and giggled. 'Are you two getting married?' she asked with the simplicity of a child.

'No,' they replied at the same time, then laughed. Maybe it really was that simple, Justine thought as they continued in silence.

Or maybe not.

Priscilla met them as they neared the house and claimed her daughter, with a look in Justine's direction that said it all.

Seriously, that woman was everywhere. Didn't she have anything better to do than to spy on other people?

10

When Justine had finished feeding Rexus the next morning, Lord Brooks was waiting for her outside the enclosure. Surprised to see him, she offered him her arm for support when she noticed him leaning heavily on his walking stick.

'Thank you, my dear. My confounded knee is giving me a little trouble today but no one likes to admit to getting old so if it's all right with you, could we just pretend that we're walking arm in arm because it gives me comfort, not because I'm falling apart?'

Justine laughed. 'Of course. We can pretend if you like, but just so you know, it gives me comfort walking with you too. It feels sort of . . . familiar.'

'Truly?' He turned to face her, his raisin-dark eyes glittering with interest.

And the usual mischief, Justine thought.

'Henry's wife rarely bothers with an old man like me. Thinks I've lost my marbles.'

'And have you?'

'Oh, on numerous occasions, but I always find them again.' This time there was no mistaking the mischief, and Lord Brooks gave her arm a little squeeze. 'So, I understand Tom has shown you the grounds, but I don't suppose you've seen my greenhouse.'

At the mention of Tom, Justine felt her face go hot, and she lowered her eyes to hide what she felt. She suspected Lord Brooks wasn't fooled anyway, but he had enough tact not to go there.

'I only saw it from the outside,' she replied. 'I was told it was off-limits.'

'Not to a sensible young lady like yourself. I just say that to keep the children out of there. My orchids don't respond so well to Henry's little darlings.'

'They're well brought up,' said Justine in defence of the girls, 'although I think Portia might have a slightly mischievous streak.'

'A *slightly* mischievous streak?' The old man scoffed. 'I dare say. I keep the greenhouse locked but I could swear someone has been in there on several occasions. It's the little things,' he added when Justine sent him a searching look — *was* he perhaps losing his marbles? — 'such as my trowel having been moved, or my Panama hat having fallen off its peg. I've raised the subject with Priscilla but she's adamant that it can't be either of the girls, and her expression always suggests that I probably misplaced them.'

'We can all be a little absent-minded now and again — ' Justine began but he interrupted her.

'I'm certainly not absent-minded!'

Justine frowned. 'Well, it could be Portia, I suppose. She doesn't miss a trick.' She remembered how Portia had proudly announced that she knew where the key for the lion enclosure had been kept before Justine asked Tom to move it.

'Exactly. As for my mind, it's never been clearer, and it's all thanks to you.'

'Me?'

He patted her hand. 'Your presence here at Stonybrook has spiced things up. How many people can say they have a lion in their back garden?'

'Not many, I would hope. It's not like living with a fox or a hedgehog!'

'And I've been watching you,' Lord Brooks continued. 'You're not afraid of working hard. That's good, I like it.'

Justine sent him a sideways look. She liked Lord Brooks, whom one could perhaps refer to as 'sprightly' except that wouldn't do him justice, but it sounded a little as if he was patronising her.

'You pick yourself up when you fall over. I like that too. You're not one of these namby-pamby spoilt young women who have a fit when they break a finger-nail or a false eyelash comes off. I cannot abide that.'

She sent him a wry grin. 'I've met people like that, and they're always townies. That's what we call non-circus folk, and you're right, I'm not like that. Life in the circus is tough, and there's no room for softness. You either sink or swim. But then again, to be fair, most women aren't as you have described.'

Lord Brooks nodded. 'Tell me about your childhood.'

'My childhood? Why?' He was the most astonishing man.

'Oh, indulge an old man. Every young boy dreams of running away with the circus. I was no different. I'm sure I'd have made an excellent clown.'

'My cousin's a clown,' said Justine.

'Is he now? Was he the clown I saw performing when I visited Circus Belmont in Ireland?'

'That would've been him, yes. I think he makes a good clown.'

'Judging by the laughs he gets, I'd say he's very good,' said Lord Brooks. 'But we're digressing. Your childhood, was it happy?'

His question threw her. Had her childhood been happy? It wasn't something she'd ever considered before.

'Well . . . ' she began, then stopped to think again. ''Happy' doesn't quite cover it. It was fantastic,' she said, and as she did, so many memories came flooding back, those moments of true bliss amidst the hard work, the injuries, the monotony of pitching the tent and doing a performance only to take it down again and drive to another town to do the same the next day. The cramped living conditions with very little privacy. The fear each time her parents went into the ring with the animals. Saying goodbye to the team at the end of every season, many of whom she might never see again. The community, the camaraderie . . . God, how she missed it! But she didn't want to talk about that now.

'It was an unusual childhood, with a massive extended family. We worked hard, even from very young, but we also found time to enjoy being together.'

'And did you get any formal education?'

'Uhm, yes, I did, but perhaps not in

the way you might understand it. When touring we'd have a couple of teachers with us, but that was mainly for the younger age groups. As we got older, there was a fair amount of distance learning. And when we overwintered, usually in the same place, we'd go to the local schools.'

'Did you find it difficult being an outsider?'

'Not really. The local kids thought we were cool and always wanted to hear more about circus life and what we'd been doing during a particular season. We weren't bullied if that's what you mean. And my cousins and I have all taken our GCSEs, plus my cousin Janos has also done A-levels and is starting agricultural college next September.'

The last she added almost defensively, she realised, because she didn't want him to think that she and her cousins were illiterate. It had become important to her that Lord Brooks thought well of her although she couldn't explain why she should feel that way. She'd never before cared about what the 'townies' thought.

As if reading her mind, he said, 'I often find that one perhaps puts a little too much emphasis on formal education. After all, it's hardly the fancy letters or titles we can put before or after our names which determine our level of intelligence.'

'I agree,' said Justine, 'but some people don't see it that way. I've been lucky it was never an issue at school, and lucky that my parents gave me the gift of self-esteem and resilience to deal with the tough times life sometimes throws at you.'

Like now, she thought, when life as she'd always known it was over, and she had to start again.

To her surprise tears appeared in Lord Brooks's eyes just like she thought had happened during the church service, and as if choked with emotion, he patted her arm lightly. 'Now, let's take a quick look at my greenhouse and then have a tour of the house. After that, I'd be delighted if you could join me for lunch in my apartment provided you're not busy. I've ordered in from the King's Arms in the village as I always do.'

This puzzled Justine. 'Don't you eat with the family?'

'Rarely,' he replied. 'I find the girls too noisy at dinner time, and when they're away at school, I find the atmosphere too strained, so a happy medium for me is to eat by myself. I will say this for Henry's wife: she does dote on her children so there are no holds barred when they're at home. Never quite understood why she chose to send them to boarding school.'

'Maybe she thought that was expected of her,' Justine suggested.

'I suppose so.' Lord Brooks shrugged, clearly uninterested in Priscilla's motives for anything.

He changed the subject, and for the rest of the walk to the greenhouse he talked about his passion for orchids and seeing things grow. 'It all started during my first visit to Kew Gardens many years ago. I was just so impressed by these plants that seemed able to grow in and on virtually everything. Their ability to adapt fascinates me. Like Buddleia that you often see growing on the brick walls of railway bridges, but more exotic. I swore I would dedicate my twilight years, as it were, to cultivating these flowers, and I've been doing so for nearly twenty years.'

'I've never had the chance to grow anything much from my own efforts,' said Justine as a wistful feeling stole over her. 'We had a few geraniums in planters on the back of the caravan, but they are my mother's doing, not mine. I grew cress on the windowsill, but that's about it.'

And how I miss those geraniums, she thought.

'Then let me show you my beauties.'

They'd arrived at the greenhouse, which was a large glass structure with a lantern roof, more like an orangery if Justine remembered the term correctly.

Attached to one of outbuildings at the back of the house, it was accessed through the long staff corridor leading from the kitchen past Tom and Henry's offices, the laundry room, and the wine cellar. Justine had never been that far towards the back of the house because it was at the opposite end to the café and her own small apartment across from it.

They entered through an outside door, locked with an old-fashioned brass key with an intricate pattern on the bow part, which hung from Lord Brooks's keyring, and Justine wondered wryly if Portia knew where the spare key was kept, if there was one.

Probably.

A wall of humidity hit them as they entered, a shock after the cold, crisp air outside, and Lord Brooks, the perfect gentleman, helped Justine out of her scarf and jacket and hung them on a coat stand by the door.

'Apologies for the temperature. Although orchids are hardy, they do prefer a more subtropical climate to the one Norfolk can provide. They especially dislike the ammonia spray the farmers around here use to fertilise their fields. Not a match made in heaven.'

He laughed at his own jokey comparison, but there was no mistaking his passion. After having showed her a few prize specimens, he picked up a small plant with purple and pale yellow variegated petals.

'This is my first successful cross-breed. I'm thinking of calling it *Phalaenopsis Elusiae Justiniae*, because growing it has eluded me for a while. How do you feel about that?'

Justine didn't know what to say to that, thinking he was being only half-serious. And what did he mean with that bit about being elusive?

'You shrug, I see,' he said. 'Perhaps you think I'm making fun of you. I can assure I'm not. I'd like to name it after you if you're in agreement.'

She cleared her throat. 'In that case I'm honoured. But why me?'

He gave a dismissive wave. 'You young people want an explanation for everything. It wasn't like that in my day. We were better at taking things at face value.'

'Don't forget I belong to the Google generation. There really *is* an explanation for practically anything.' She smiled. 'But I appreciate the gesture. No one's ever named a flower after me.'

'There's a perfectly good explanation. But I'll come to that. Let's close up here, and I'll show you the parts of the house that I'm sure you haven't seen yet. Come, my dear.'

Again she lent him her arm, and they left the conservatory through the connecting door to the house, which Lord Brooks locked carefully after him.

Then he proceeded to show her everything on the ground floor that she hadn't seen already: the games room, which housed an enormous billiard table, and the wine cellar with the numerous bottles of fine wine he'd collected over the years.

'When I still travelled, I'd visit vineyards in France and Italy, and some of these wines will soon be at their optimum for drinking.'

Not knowing anything whatsoever about fine wines, Justine nodded as she ran her hands over the yellowed wine labels. Some were at least twenty years old, and many of them were older than that, and she presumed that the youngest of the wines came from the time Lord Brooks stopped travelling.

He confirmed this with his next words. 'That was when I stopped going abroad. Didn't seem quite the same buying my wine from wine merchants here.'

A shadow passed across his face, and Justine wondered if he lost his interest in the collection around the time of his eldest son's death, but she was unsure about the dates.

He then showed her the living areas on the ground floor, including the smaller of the two sitting rooms. This room she'd already been inside when she was introduced to Henry and his family for the first time. She recalled Priscilla's hostile reaction to her and shivered briefly.

What was it with that woman?

As they went through the double glass doors with the engraved birds, she experienced again a sense of familiarity, much like the one she'd had at the time of the Christmas party. The image of her hand pushing it open puzzled her. One winter she and her parents as well as her uncle and aunt had stayed in a small manor house in County Kildare in Ireland, housesitting because the owner was in hospital. She remembered now that the house in Ireland had had glass doors like these, some of them engraved.

That must be where the memory came from.

After the living areas on the ground floor, Lord Brooks led her up the central staircase, with a running commentary on who the different people in the portraits were, something she'd only guessed at on her first and only trip up the stairs.

'That's me,' he said and pointed to the painting of himself in clothes of a different decade, but this she'd known the last time she had looked at the portrait.

He'd lost most of his hair, and what was left had turned an elegant shade of quicksilver, but the face and the eyes were the same, as dark and penetrating as those of the live model beside her.

'And that was my wife.' He indicated the painting next to his own portrait, the one Justine had been studying when Priscilla had interrupted her and told her she was intruding on the family's privacy. This had enraged her; she understood more than anyone the need for privacy, not having had much when growing up.

The woman was blonde with cat-like slanted green eyes, revealing a dreamy yet determined expression, her cheek-bones high but delicately sculptured, and her mouth was half-turned upwards in an almost Mona Lisa-like smile, but with more smile and less mystery.

The mystery was the emotion her face invoked in Justine, a feeling of wanting to like her and already knowing her at the same time.

Her throat went suddenly dry and her hands clammy as a feeling of recognition snaked down her spine, icily and uncontrollably. With her knees almost buckling under her, she turned to Lord Brooks with a silent question.

'She was the love of my life,' he said softly as he watched her closely, 'and you're the spitting image of her. She is, of course, your grandmother.'

11

'Yes,' he said. 'You are my granddaughter.'

'What?' A thousand thoughts flitted through Justine's mind, questions of how and when and what had happened, but she kept returning to the 'why'.

'Oh come on, that's just completely ridiculous! Just because I look like someone in a portrait, that doesn't mean anything. They say everyone has a double out there in the world somewhere. Have you . . . ' She bit her lip, realising that she was just about to accuse him of losing it.

He bristled. 'No, I haven't lost my mind. It isn't just a random resemblance, there's a story behind it. A sad one.'

'I don't understand,' she said. 'Did my father run away with the circus, and you pretended he was dead? Did you pretend that we were all dead?'

'No, you've got the wrong end of the stick. It's more complicated than that, and sinister.'

'Sinister?' A sudden anger welled up in her. 'What did he do?'

'I'll tell you everything. But not here.' They still stood near the top of the stairs in front of the portraits, and although they were completely alone, Justine felt rather than saw a slight shadow below, but it was gone so quickly it could have been her imagination.

Or the cat, maybe.

'We'll go to my apartments, as we'd agreed. There I'll answer all your questions. Please, I'd much appreciate it if you would lend an old man your arm again.'

Justine did as he asked but realised when they reached Lord Brooks's section of the house that she'd been leaning on him as much as he'd been leaning on her.

Ignoring the lunch that had been laid

out for them, perhaps by the pub staff — certainly not Priscilla — he went straight to the drinks cabinet and poured them both a brandy. Wordlessly, Justine took a large gulp then wrapped her fingers around the brandy snifter, grateful for the sensation of heat spreading in her chest. So many questions, each with different feelings attached, but mostly the sense of something falling into place in her head.

Painfully so.

I've always known.

'Please tell me what happened. Are my parents not my parents?' she asked when she was finally able to speak.

'Not biologically. You're the only child of my eldest son Edward, Henry's uncle. As I'm sure Tom must have told you, Edward died in a drowning accident with his wife and child — you — when the tide came in too fast. At least that's the official version.'

'What's the unofficial version?' Justine swallowed hard, knowing that she had to hear the truth even as she feared it. 'Did my parents, I mean, Mum and Dad, abduct me?'

There'd been stories in the news about abducted children who'd never been found, and of how the natural parents clung to the hope that they were still alive and living happily with another family somewhere in the world. Rather than facing the unbearable reality that the child was dead. She completely understood that.

'It's a little closer to actual events,' said Lord Brooks, whom she supposed she'd have to think of as her grandfather now although she was far from ready to call him 'Granddad' yet. 'It's a tale of murder,' he continued.

'Murder?' Black spots appeared before her eyes, and she gulped down the rest of her brandy, only to succumb to an excruciating coughing fit. The cough restored her, and she put her empty glass down with a clunk. 'I think it's time you told me everything from the beginning. Don't bother trying to shield me; I'm over the shock now.'

Lord Brooks nodded, admiration clearly visible in his dark eyes. 'Very well. It was a classic case of sibling rivalry. I adored my sons, both my wife and I did, and they had everything we were able to give them. But only one could inherit the manor and the parkland. You can't split it. You can divide the farmland, and the other can have the home farm. That was to be George's upon my death, but he wasn't happy with this. Even from a very young age he saw himself as having been 'short-changed' by birth. I'm afraid it ate away at him.

'It was the little things at first; a favourite toy mysteriously broken, a punctured bicycle tyre, things like that; innocent enough in themselves, except I came to suspect they were deliberate. My wife did not agree, thought everything entirely accidental. That was the first and last time we ever disagreed on anything.'

He paused and took a sip of his brandy, a faraway look in his eyes as he stared out over the lawn at the front of the house. Justine wished he'd just get on with it.

After what seemed like an age he picked up his story again. 'It then escalated as the boys grew older. Missing car keys, pieces of glass in food, a loose saddle, things like that.'

Justine remembered her fall when her saddle slipped — had that been an accident or deliberate?

But who could have done it if it *was* deliberate?

Lord Brooks didn't seem to have noticed and continued. 'This was after the boys returned from school. I'd insisted that one went to Harrow and the other Eton, by the way. Then the pranks became malicious and dangerous. I tried to take Edward into my confidence but he merely thought me paranoid. He and George did a lot together, you know the sort of thing young men do: partying, double-dating since there were only two years between them, going to the races, and even working on the estate together. In the end I thought it had stopped.

'Then George met a lovely woman and married her. Edward married soon after but George was the first to have a child, Henry of course. This was the first time he actually seemed pleased with his lot, that *he* had a son and Edward no children. I thought he'd got over his jealousy.'

He turned back to Justine. 'But then later you were born. Mary Elizabeth Brooks, named after two English queens. Edward now had a child as well, and although you were 'only' a daughter, Edward still stood to inherit the manor. George began to focus on you. This time Edward did believe me.' He smiled suddenly, and the darkness left his face. 'You were a beautiful baby. Plump and content, and always had a happy smile from the moment you were able to.'

'What happened?'

'Well, my daughter-in-law, Isobel, rarely left you unattended. Both she and Edward had come to realise what was going on. Even so, once you were found with the covers in your cot pulled up over your face and tucked tightly in, which was clearly not an accident. Another time a swarm of bees found their way into the nursery, and once you were older and able to walk, the nanny found you in the woods by the lake after she'd gone for a loo break.'

A shiver ran down Justine's spine; it was beginning to dawn on her that she was lucky to be alive. 'So, my parents sent me away for my own protection?'

Lord Brooks shook his head. 'We had no proof, and your grandmother still wouldn't hear a word against George. In the end he was sent away, to manage another property we had in Devon, from my wife's family, and life returned to normal. Your mother became pregnant again, and I was preoccupied because my beloved wife was showing signs of dementia. That was when the accident happened. A rapidly rising tide, and Edward's car was swept out to sea with all of you in it. The bodies were never found.'

'But I survived.'

Her grandfather nodded.

'How?'

'The Belmonts,' he replied simply.

'My parents?'

He nodded again. 'Your parents were out sailing at the time and saw it happen. Your mother, Beth Belmont I mean, swam to the car to help, but Edward and his wife were already dead — how we'll never know. You were still alive on the back seat, and she got you out before it was too late. And — '

'Why was I not brought home?' Justine interrupted.

Her grandfather was silent for a while, his hands twitching as if of their own accord. 'This is very difficult for me, you understand, but from their rented sailing boat your parents had witnessed the accident. Another car, a powerful Jeep exactly like the one George was driving in those days, was pushing Edward's car toward the incoming tide until the sea took it. Your parents could do nothing from their boat except watch in horror and then try to rescue the passengers when the Jeep drove off.'

Justine's head was still bursting with questions. 'They never reported it. Why? George murdered my parents.'

'Yes, he did. I have no doubt it was George, although your parents were too far away to read the number plate.' Her grandfather wiped away a tear that had trickled down his cheek. 'The simple answer is, they adored you.'

'Did they know me?'

'The year you were two, Circus Belmont came to the village and did several performances. Because of my old fascination with the circus I'd let them pitch the tent — the 'big top' I think you people call it — on my field for free, and they kindly gave us permission to see behind the scenes showing us the animals among other things. Even then you seemed to have an affinity with big cats and weren't afraid of them at all. Edward and Isobel became friends with the Belmonts. They had had lunch together on the boat that day, shortly before the accident. That's why they were nearby. When they witnessed that atrocious act, they took you away to keep you safe.'

Justine tried to stop tears from welling up.

'A couple of years later their conscience got the better of them, and they contacted me. I arranged to meet them at a motorway service station, intrigued at what they might have to tell me. They confessed to what they'd witnessed and to whisking you away. At first I didn't believe them and thought they were charlatans hoping to get some money out of a sentimental old man — take a couple of years, and one toddler can be made to look like another easily enough. But when Beth Belmont showed me a piece of muslin, I recognised the embroidered initials as my wife's craftsmanship, and knew they were speaking the truth. A DNA test would have confirmed it, but I didn't need one.

'I'm afraid I was very angry at first and threatened them with the police, but seeing how protective they were and how contented you seemed, it occurred to me that for you to grow up in a circus wasn't a bad thing. You'd be safely tucked away from George who was unaware you were still alive, and we agreed that you'd be brought back when the time was right.'

So that was what her father had meant when he'd said it was time she went her own way. He knew she had to go back.

Her grandfather continued. 'After their revelation I was unsure what to do about George. The Belmonts agreed they'd tell the police what had happened, if I asked it of them, reluctantly because that would mean giving you up. But since there was no definite proof, if we failed to reach a conviction, that would put you right back in the firing line again. And the Belmonts would probably have gone to prison and that seemed wrong to me after they'd saved your life. So I let George work on the estate while I pondered what was best. He had a beautiful and sensible wife, and he was still my son. To give him his due, he was a conscientious steward, as is Henry, and always had the best interest of the estate in mind.'

'I can't imagine Henry being anything else,' said Justine and meant it. Her cousin . . . Henry was her cousin, and Gabi, Sara, and Janos weren't.

'I made sure I changed my will,' said her grandfather. 'George knew nothing of this, and sadly some years after he died of cancer, and after Henry married that social climber, Priscilla. It was then that I told Henry that I'd made some changes to my will, and that I still hadn't decided what would happen to the manor. He took it with his usual grace, but that's Henry for you. Generous to a fault. When I die, some of this will be yours, the daughter of my first-born son. Just as it should be.'

He beamed at her, and having shifted the burden of responsibility onto the next generation, appeared suddenly younger. The unexpected burden settled on Justine's shoulders like a heavy cloak, and suddenly it was all too much.

The temptation to get up and leave and never come back propelled her physically out of her chair, but instead of heading for the door as she'd feared her feet might do of their own volition, she went to stand by the window.

A mist had descended over the lawns, and everything seemed to have stopped as if someone had pressed a button. The only movement was Portia running across the lawn and casting a furtive glance behind her.

Justine smiled wryly. The girl was clearly trying to escape her mother's loving control again. Who could blame her?

The thought of Priscilla brought her mind back to Henry. How would he feel about her? Would he resent her and see her as having wormed her way into their grandfather's affection for money? She really hoped not; she'd come to like and respect Henry, and if she was going to be part of this, she'd need his help and acceptance.

The temptation to turn tail was overwhelming, to wash her hands of it all.

Another part of her, smaller perhaps, began to swell with pride. She was made of sterner stuff, and despite her confusion and anger, an anger directed at both her adoptive parents as well as at her grandfather, she knew she wasn't going to turn her back on the old man.

Another thought slithered into her conscious mind.

Tom.

Had he known all along and had sweet-talked her into falling in love with him so *he* could get a slice of the pie?

If so, he'd succeeded. It had come on so slowly that she'd hardly noticed, had even pushed the thought aside when it intruded too much, but there was no denying that he'd become very important to her.

She turned sharply. 'I'll do it. I will accept the responsibility placed upon me by birth, but I want complete openness and honesty from now on. No more dark secrets.'

As the last of the deep lines seemed to disappear from her grandfather's face, she softened a little. 'But I'll need some help.'

And if Tom had played her false, then there would be hell to pay.

12

'So what do we do now?' Justine asked.

Still reeling from the impact of what she'd just been told, she sat down again with her hands in her lap, willing them to stop shaking. A mixture of apprehension and excitement coursed through her, tinged with sadness for the biological parents she had never got to know. And sadness for George too, for the madness which had driven him to do what he did. A murderer should pay for his crime, and George already had, with his life. Poetic justice perhaps, that he didn't get to see his grandchildren grow up, just as Justine had been deprived too.

And yet, in many ways, she hadn't suffered any deprivation at all, because she'd had a happy and uncomplicated life up until now. She wanted to hold onto that.

'Well, I find one thinks best on a full stomach,' her grandfather replied, 'so let's have this delicious lunch the pub has laid on for us. Although I fear the chicken pie may have gone cold.'

'I'll sort it out,' said Justine. She'd noticed a small kitchen just as they'd entered her grandfather's apartments, and she took the two plates of pie, mash and vegetables in there to reheat the plates gently in the oven.

When she returned, her grandfather had poured them both a glass of cider.

'Brewed locally,' he explained, 'and good old-fashioned stuff. Not this new-fangled nonsense which tastes like lemonade.'

Justine laughed in spite of herself. She was going to enjoy having a grandfather as she'd never had any grandparents at all. Her cousins had their Hungarian grandmother who would spit and mutter curses in her own language when she was displeased with something. Which was often.

'I expect you'd like to talk to your

parents,' said her grandfather.

Damn right. 'They're on holiday.'

He shook his head. 'They're staying in the village. At the pub.'

More machinations behind her back? Justine narrowed her eyes at him.

He shrugged. 'We agreed that they would be nearby when I told you about your ancestry.'

'And a whole lot more than just my ancestry,' she commented dryly. 'Like murder.'

'Yes, a whole lot more. They'll be able to tell you the rest and advise you on what to do. They're your parents after all and know you better than I do.' A sad smile crossed his features.

Justine put her hand on his arm. Although her grandfather had sprung a massive revelation on her, at least he'd been honest with her, and her affection for the old guy grew.

'We'll soon get to know each other as well,' she reassured him.

* * *

Anxious to see her parents, Justine left him soon after lunch. Her grandfather was right, she mused as she made her way to the village; everything was easier on a full stomach. Her mind had cleared. Yes, she was still plagued by doubts, not about knowing the truth but whether she could ever live up to what was expected of her. Her future would be so completely different from what she'd ever imagined, and she hardly knew where to begin.

Her parents — Elijah and Beth, Mum and Dad — were waiting for her at the King's Arms, in a booth in a quiet corner sheltered by high-backed tweed-covered benches. They rose as she approached, and her mother stepped forward as if to hug her, then let her arms drop, uncertain.

'So, he's told you,' her father said simply.

She nodded. The earlier anger returned, and with it the urge to fling all manner of accusations at her parents, but their faces, so contrite and hopeful, and so full of love, stopped her. How could you accuse someone of having saved your life and of giving you the most exciting existence imaginable? More exciting than growing up at Stonybrook, she had no doubts about that.

Instead she hugged her mother and gave her father her hand. He brought it to his cheek and kissed it.

Blood was one thing, family was another.

But there were still so many unanswered questions and she needed all the answers now if she was to make sense of her future.

They all sat down in the booth again, and Elijah ordered coffee for them all. 'I expect you have some questions for us.'

Where to begin? Justine unwound her scarf and tossed both that and her jacket on the seat beside her, then cleared her throat and started with the most pressing. 'What exactly happened that day?'

'It's a long story so let me start at the beginning. We'd been offered the use of

Lord Brooks's field for free, so obviously we accepted that since keeping our overheads down has always been important. Consequently there was a lot of coming and going between some folks on the back lot and Stonybrook. Edward and his wife, Isobel, were fascinated with our way of life, and would often come to visit us after a performance. I guess we became friends, despite our very different backgrounds.'

'She was a very nice lady, your mother,' Beth added, and Justine took her hand.

'*You* are my mother.'

Tears of joy sprang into Beth's eyes, but not being one for great shows of emotion, she quickly blinked them away.

'We couldn't have children. Jethro and Yolande already had Gabi and Janos, but there were no girls yet, and you just stole our hearts immediately. We'd thought of adopting but with our itinerant lifestyle and a dangerous job, I seriously doubt any adoption agency would have considered us suitable.

'One evening after a fantastic performance Edward came to celebrate with us at the back lot. After a few drinks he pulled me to one side and told me he was afraid something would happen to him.'

The barmaid arrived with their coffees, and Elijah stopped, then continued again where he'd left off. 'At first I thought he was bonkers, but when he went into more detail and explained about his brother, I could see that he was serious. He made us promise to take care of you if anything *should* happen to him.' Elijah shook his head. 'I'm not quite sure how he imagined that was going to pan out — did he think we'd just steal you away? Good luck trying to explain that to the judge!'

'But we understood his fears,' Beth interjected, 'however irrational it all seemed. And we promised. After all, it's easy enough to make promises when you don't think what you're promising will become relevant.'

'And when it happened just as he'd

feared . . . ' Elijah frowned and stirred cream into his coffee.

Beth squeezed Justine's hand. 'Such a shock . . . '

Justine squeezed her mother's hand in return. 'But you saved me.'

Beth nodded. 'And we kept our promise.'

'Although we had to let Lord Brooks know. Couldn't let him think you'd perished in that car. He's your grandfather after all, and Edward had told us his father knew about the attempts on his life.'

'He told me he didn't believe you at first,' said Justine.

'We knew he wouldn't. A lot of townies have preconceived ideas about circus people: that being itinerant means we're dishonest for instance. But you had this on you.'

Elijah took a piece of cloth out of his coat pocket and handed it to her. The loosely woven cotton square, or what was left of it, was old and frayed, and one corner appeared to have been cut with a pair of scissors — the tiny square she had sewn into her costume, she realised with a jolt — but the pale pink initials 'MEB' in another corner were still readable.

'Your security blanket when you were very small.'

'You were so sweet the way you used to cling to it,' Beth whispered.

'We hoped your grandfather would understand that we did this because Edward had asked us to, not because we were criminals.'

'And that we already loved you,' her mother added.

'He did understand,' said Justine, 'and I'm glad that he let me stay with you. You'll always be my parents.'

Beth eyes welled up again, and this time she didn't try to hide her emotions. 'You've forgiven us?'

'There's nothing to forgive. George was the one who did wrong, and George is dead. But my life has changed overnight, and there's a lot I need to understand about myself.'

'We know,' said Elijah, 'and we'll help you in any way we can.'

'If you'll let us,' said Beth.

Justine reached across and took her father's hand in addition to her mother's. 'Of course I will, but in the first instance this is something I need to work through myself.'

The pretty barmaid returned to ask if everything was all right.

'This is a rather charming village,' said Elijah, with a glint in his eye after the woman had left again. 'We might consider overwintering here.'

'Oh, you!' Beth prodded him with her elbow, and they both grinned.

The laughter provided a healthy antidote to the heavy subject matter, but Justine knew, as did her parents, that it would take a long time before she'd recover from the shock, if she ever would. After all, a whole lifetime of lies had yet to be untangled.

* * *

She left her parents an hour later, having reassured them that while she appreciated their offer of help, she had to come to terms in her own head first with this different life which awaited; this whole new set of responsibilities.

First Lord Brooks had to tell the rest of the family, which they'd agreed he'd do when she returned from the pub. Then they had to deal with the inevitable fall-out that she suspected would be on a massive scale. She was robbing Henry of his inheritance. Even though she was the daughter of the first-born, Henry was nine years older than her, *and* male, which would be of significance to anyone taking a more old-fashioned stance.

She was certain Priscilla would look at it that way.

Then she had to figure out how Tom fit into all of this and how much he already knew. She wasn't sure she trusted her own judgment when it came to him.

Irony would have it that Tom was the first person she met when she returned. She tried schooling her features into a neutral expression, not very successfully, because Tom immediately sensed something was up.

'Are you all right?' he asked. 'You look as if you've seen a ghost.'

I'm the ghost, she thought. The child returned from the dead.

When she shook her head, he put his hands on her shoulders. 'If anyone's upset you, I'll — '

'How much do you really know about me?' she blurted out, having decided on the spur of the moment that attack was the best defence.

'*Know* about you?' The question clearly took him by surprise, and his surprise told Justine everything she needed to know. Tom knew nothing of her background other than what he'd been presented with. His affection and kindness towards her must be genuine. She breathed a sigh of relief.

Tom was frowning. 'That's a peculiar

question. I think I know what I need to know, that you're beautiful and talented. That you're kind and tolerant towards other people even when they don't deserve it.'

'Anything else?' Her eyes were firmly fixed on his face, searching for signs of duplicity.

'That you sit well on a horse, and that you can scratch a lion behind the ears and live to tell the tale.' He grinned foolishly and smoothed a strand of her hair behind her ear.

'Be serious, now.'

'I know how important you are to me. Whatever else there is to know about you, I look forward to finding out. It won't change the way I feel about you. Does that answer your question?'

She let him pull her close. He smelled, as he always did, faintly of horses and fresh air, and she buried her face against his chest with a sense that she'd somehow come home. So much had happened in the span of a few weeks, but Tom had steadfastly remained the same apart from his initial suspicion of her. Whatever happened from now on, she hoped that, at least, wouldn't change.

* * *

'Doesn't look like you two need the blessing of an old man, I think.'

Tom let go of Justine when Richard appeared on the front steps of the house. It was perhaps a little embarrassing for them to be caught almost *in flagrante*, as it were, but when he'd seen the expression on Justine's face as she walked up the drive, his first and only thought had been to ease whatever was troubling her in whichever way he could.

Because it was clear that something had shocked her. He hoped it wasn't something Priscilla had said — if so, he'd have words with her, Henry's wife or not.

It hadn't occurred to him that they were standing in full view of the house.

'Sorry,' he said.

Richard waved his hand dismissively. 'Don't be sorry, my friend. I've been observing the two of you for some time and have been meaning to tell you both that I approve of your choice.'

'Thank you.' Tom grinned when he noticed Justine turn red; she wasn't as used to the old man's outspokenness as he was.

Richard turned to Justine, and an uncharacteristic seriousness crept over his face. 'Ready, my dear?'

Tom looked from one to the other. He'd been right, something was definitely a little off. 'Ready for what? What's going on?'

'I have something to tell you all. Come, Henry and Priscilla are already in the drawing room.'

As they walked back through the house, Tom glanced at Justine, but her face gave nothing away other than wanting to get it over with. Whatever *it* was.

In the formal drawing room Priscilla was pacing in front of the large windows overlooking the park, an air of irritation in her stride. Henry was his usual self, seated in a chair with his back to his wife. He rolled his eyes at Tom when the three of them entered. His expression was saying 'What's the old man cooking up now?'.

Tom smiled, as ever grateful for his cousin's even temper, such a contrast to his wife's. They said that opposites attract, but in Tom's opinion a couple could be too different from each other.

The old man sat down, but Justine remained standing beside him as if to shelter him, Tom thought.

'What's this about?' Priscilla asked, her tone as brittle as frost.

'You're probably wondering why I've called you here,' said Richard, ignoring her outburst. 'I have something to tell you, and it relates to my will — '

'What's *she* doing here, then?' Priscilla stabbed a finger in Justine's direction, but Tom thought he detected a hint of resignation in her voice. Which was odd; Priscilla wasn't known for resigning herself to anything.

I'm probably wrong, he thought, but a tight feeling began gripping his chest and wouldn't let go.

'It relates to her too,' replied Richard mildly. 'In fact, the reason we're here is entirely because of her.'

Priscilla opened her mouth to say something, but instead sent Justine a look that could have floored an elephant. Henry glanced at Justine with sudden interest, recognition even.

'Justine is my granddaughter,' the old man continued.

The room fell into stunned silence. Priscilla sagged and gaped at Justine, and Tom gripped the back of the chair Richard was sitting on, turning his knuckles white, but Henry looked right at Justine, studying her features carefully, then he nodded as if to himself.

'There *is* a likeness to my grandmother,' he said, then turned to his grandfather with a frown and demanded, almost angrily, 'But how is this possible? What's the connection?'

The tightness in Tom's chest deepened as Justine spoke for the first time.

'Edward was my father. He . . . my parents . . . ' She faltered and glanced at the old man who gave her an encouraging nod. 'My foster parents, the Belmonts, er, witnessed the accident when the tide came in and tried to rescue everyone but I was the only one still alive. They were childless and decided to keep me. They only told Lord Br — our grandfather later.'

It sounded plausible. Tom had noticed a lack of resemblance to her parents the day he met her, but hadn't thought about it further. This would explain it. But he was certain there was more to this than Justine and the old man were letting on. It was almost as if they were in cahoots over something they weren't telling.

'Good God!' Priscilla gave a short bark of laughter. 'I've heard some fibs in my time, but this one beats them all hands down. How did you manage to persuade that old fool that you're his long lost granddaughter? What a load of rubbish!'

'Priscilla!' Henry cut back to his wife, clearly aghast to hear her speak like that, then he rose and crossed the room to take Justine's hands in his.

Tom's throat closed up; he should be doing this, he should be the one to welcome Justine into the family despite his own tenuous link to it, but he found himself unable to move, to speak even.

'I see it clearly now,' said Henry, a catch in his voice. 'I've passed that portrait of my grandmother on the stairs many times a day, and since you came here, something has made me stop and look at her more closely. Now I know why I did that.' He smiled. 'You're my cousin, then. I can't begin to explain how happy that makes me.'

Justine welcomed her cousin's embrace, at first a little tentatively it seemed, then with genuine gratitude. Tom's heart contracted painfully — this must be so difficult for her but she bore it with the stoicism he'd come to admire.

Henry let go of his newfound cousin and beamed down at her. Tom noticed Justine swallow hard.

'Oh, come on, Henry!' Priscilla hissed. 'Don't tell me you're buying into this crap. This impostor has you all wrapped around her little finger. You need to grow a flipping backbone!'

'Yes, I do,' Henry replied. 'Which is why, for once, I'd like you to shut up! What Justine has told us is more than plausible. Seeing the resemblance, I believe it to be the truth.'

But Priscilla wasn't to be silenced that easily. 'You're so desperate to leave here, Henry, that anyone with the tiniest bit of family resemblance could just come and snatch away your inheritance. You don't care about that at all. You don't care about your family, me and the girls.'

'As I've told you before, it's not *my* inheritance, and it never will be, certainly not now.'

'Well, I demand a DNA test,' his wife went on, impervious to the dark look

Henry sent her.

Tom noticed Richard shudder and put a hand on his shoulder, just as the old man reached for Justine's hand.

'Would you consent to that, my dear? A DNA test?'

Justine nodded briefly. Tom thought she looked tired.

'Of course she'd say that,' snapped Priscilla. 'She'll do anything to get her hands on an inheritance I know she can't possibly be entitled to. Like I said, she has you wrapped — '

Her tirade was interrupted as the door flung open and Portia appeared, tear-stricken and streaked with grime.

'You need to come now! Dilly's fallen into the lion's cage!'

13

Justine didn't hesitate. She left the room and ran across the lawn to the lion's enclosure.

'Wait!' Tom caught up with her. 'You're going to need help. And I've got the key.'

She nodded. 'You get to Cordelia while I try to distract Rexus. He's tame, but . . . '

She didn't finish the sentence. No need. They both knew there was a real danger that Rexus, however tame he was, could attack the child if he became stressed or felt threatened in any way.

They reached the enclosure just as Henry and Priscilla pulled up in Tom's Jeep, which he'd left at the front of the house with the keys in the ignition. The tyres marked the grass from Henry's abrupt braking. Clasping Portia tightly by the hand, Priscilla was weeping quietly as if instinct told her that big shows of emotion could startle the lion. Henry's face was grim but calm as he helped his grandfather out of the Jeep, the old man pale from shock. Portia clung to her mother, shaking and with tears streaming down her face.

'Mummy, I'm so sorry, Mummy! I'm so sorry,' she cried over and over again.

Cordelia lay on the ground in the centre of the enclosure, not moving. The branch overhanging part of the enclosure had snapped and was only partially attached to the tree trunk, its insides sticking out like a jagged tooth. Rexus stood on the other side of the fallen branch that still separated him from the girl.

Justine's heart jumped in her chest as she took the key from Tom without a word and let herself into the enclosure.

Was she too late?

When she entered, Rexus turned to her with an ear-splitting roar, his tail swinging furiously.

'Easy, boy, easy,' she said, with a calmness she didn't feel. Her father was the lion-tamer, not her, and she racked her brains to think of what Elijah would do in a situation like this.

A stick. She needed a stick.

Backing slowly towards the fence with Rexus following her and leaving Cordelia motionless on the ground, she called quietly to Tom over her shoulder while keeping her eyes on the lion. Pacing up and down in front of her, Rexus grunted and shook his mane, something he did when uncertain or anxious about something.

'Richard's walking stick, has he got it with him?'

Henry beat his cousin to it. 'Please, save my little girl,' he beseeched as he passed the walking stick through the fence to her.

'I will.'

And she would, whatever the cost to herself. It was all her fault for showing off, for boasting that she could make Rexus count; her fault for putting ideas into Cordelia's head. She hadn't factored in a child's curiosity and need to show her parents how clever she was — she should've known better, having been like that herself as a child, thinking she could do everything and showing off her skills to the open-mouthed local schoolchildren. Any sanctions by her parents she had regarded as an inconvenience rather than reasons for caution.

And now Cordelia was in danger because of Justine's own lack of forethought.

She pointed the walking stick to where she wanted Rexus to go, just as her father would have done, and away from where Cordelia lay. 'Rexus! *Platz!*' The lion snarled and swiped at the stick but she held it out of his reach. '*Platz!*' she repeated.

Holding her breath, she kept her eyes locked with Rexus's to show the lion who was in command and inched further away from where Cordelia lay. Just as she thought he was ready to follow, the lion charged and with a growl ripped the stick from her hand with his giant paw, snapping it in half.

A searing pain tore through her arm, and behind her Portia screamed.

'Keep her quiet,' she managed to say, almost blinded by the pain and the sensation of blood gushing from her arm.

Out of the corner of her eye she saw Tom slip through the gate and crouch by Cordelia. Justine turned the lion's attention back on herself. Rexus was still pacing up and down in front of her, unsure of himself and therefore at his most dangerous, but his attention had been diverted away from Cordelia. She had to give Tom enough time to get the girl to safety, and therefore she needed to hold the lion's attention.

She wrapped her injured arm in her scarf and picked up a twig that had broken off the branch as it fell, pointing it to the ground.

'Rexus! *Platz!*' she commanded again, wincing with pain and feeling faint.

Growling, Rexus swung his tail from side to side. Justine swallowed. If he attacked again, she doubted she'd be able to hold him off, and he was now between her and the gate. Behind him she saw that Tom had Cordelia in his arms and was moving towards the gate slowly. Watching her intently, the whites of his eyes showing, Rexus hadn't noticed. She had to keep it that way, but one false move from Tom, and the lion might go for him and Cordelia instead.

There was no way of predicting what he would do. Justine was not her father, and right now she was out of her element.

Then she had an idea. Sidling further along the fence, keeping Rexus's focus on her, she made her way to the large boulder and tapped it with the twig.

'Here, Rexus. Go on, sit.'

The lion grunted.

'Come on, boy. You know you want to.'

He grunted again then crouched in attack position. The hairs stood up on the back of Justine's neck, and something dropped in her stomach as she held her breath.

The air stood still. The faces on the other side of the fence froze in horror, sweat dripped from the tip of Justine's nose, and her knees turned to jelly as she stared death right in the eyes.

Then with a whoosh Rexus was in the air and jumped . . . over her head to land on the boulder. With a good-natured sound he wrapped his tail over his front paws decorously as he'd learned to do at the circus.

A collective sigh escaped those on the outside of the fence, and the tightness in Justine's chest eased a little.

'Good boy,' she croaked. 'Good boy.' She continued to talk in a soothing voice as she lay down the twig she'd been holding and backed away slowly towards the gate. Once outside she breathed a sigh of relief. She knew Rexus, had grown up with him, but all animals could be unpredictable if startled. The branch snapping off the tree like that would have been enough to unsettle the lion in his new home.

But how come the branch had been

able to take her weight and not Cordelia's? The child was as light as a feather. Had someone tampered with it? Priscilla? She'd been in the stables when Coco's saddle straps had broken, and Justine remembered Tom's concern when he'd checked the saddle after her fall. Had Priscilla tampered with the straps that day?

'You're injured.' Tom's arm slid around her for support.

'Not seriously, I think.'

'Not seriously? You're bleeding all over the place!'

'Am I?' Justine looked at her arm as if it didn't belong to her. Only then did the pain return and she felt her knees give way. Then the world around her faded and went dark.

* * *

Tom was the first person she saw when she opened her eyes. Then the clinical surroundings and the large bandage on her right arm.

'I'm in . . . hospital?' she mumbled.

He took her hand, the uninjured one. 'You gave us all a scare. When Rexus lunged for you, he cut deep into your arm. He didn't sever your artery, but it was close. And you're going to have a noticeable scar there when your stitches come out.'

'I passed out?' Justine tried to swallow but her throat was bone dry. Tom noticed and held up a cup with a straw for her to drink. The cool water kick-started her brain again. 'How feeble of me.' She grimaced.

'Not feeble. A lesser person would've kicked up a real fuss, but you . . . there's so much strength in you. Don't ever think differently.'

'Is Cordelia all right?'

'Dilly's fine. A bump on the head the size of an egg, but otherwise she's absolutely fine. Thanks to you. If you hadn't put yourself between her and Rexus, then I think the lion could well have harmed her.'

For some reason his faith in her

embarrassed her. 'Where's Rexus now?' she asked to change the subject. 'You haven't . . . hurt him, have you?'

Tom smiled. 'Of course not. He's in his enclosure, looking suitably shame-faced. As he should.'

Justine managed to laugh at that. 'It wouldn't be the first time. He's swiped at my father a few times — ' the words 'my father' sounded strange to her ears, ' — but never injured anyone before. He must've been very stressed out to do that.'

'I think you're right,' said Tom. 'I'd noticed that he hadn't settled completely, and that branch coming down, well . . . '

No need to go over the ifs and buts. She was safe. Cordelia was safe. But the question of how it happened was bugging her.

'That branch was fairly thick,' she pointed out. 'It could take my weight, no problem, so why not Cordelia's?'

Tom regarded her thoughtfully, which frustrated her because she sensed he was holding back on her, then he got up and went into the hall for a moment. He returned with Henry and his family as well as her grandfather and pulled up a chair for the old man to sit on beside her bed. The others clustered around the foot end, their expressions grave.

Cordelia pulled away from her father and almost threw herself onto Justine. She winced in pain but couldn't bring herself to tell the little girl that she had hurt her.

'You're so brave!' cried Cordelia. 'You're the bravest person in the whole wide world! When I fell down and hurt my head, I was going to cry but Portia told me to pretend I was dead so the lion wouldn't eat me. I did but I was really scared the whole time! And then you saved me.'

Touched, Justine lifted her good hand and stroked Cordelia's soft, dark hair, just above a nasty red bump. 'You're very brave, to do that. And Portia is very clever, to think of it.'

Yes, clever indeed.

Her eyes met Tom's. 'The branch,' he said and turned to Priscilla, who was holding Portia by the hand. The older girl's face was still streaked with tears and grime that no one had thought to wipe off. 'How could it have come down?'

Justine looked at Portia, and a cold, hard lump formed in the pit of her stomach at the thought that the girl might have done something to that branch. She was certainly clever enough and knew where the tools were kept, but did she have the ability?

'I don't know.' Portia sniffed and wiped her nose with the back of her hand. 'Dilly said you'd shown her how to line-dance. So I wanted to show her that I could make the lion count, but when I got up there, it didn't feel safe and I got really scared. I didn't dare climb to the end. But Dilly did and . . . then it broke.'

That explained it. Justine wasn't heavy, but she was lighter than the combined weight of the two girls. The branch had never been as secure as she'd initially thought, and because of her negligence two little girls could have been injured or even killed. How could she ever make up for that? It's *my* fault, Justine wanted to say. *I was careless*.

Priscilla, her bottom lip trembling, stepped forward, pushing her eldest daughter ahead of her. 'How can I ever thank you? I feel so ashamed.' She took a deep, shaky breath and continued. 'For a long time I've been obsessed with the fact that Henry might not inherit Stonybrook. I thought it unfair since there was no other heir, crazy even, because this was the only way it could stay in the family, and who wouldn't want that? Or so I thought.'

'The portrait,' said Justine. 'Did you guess who I was because of the likeness?'

'No, it never occurred to me,' she replied. 'But Portia did, and because the issue of the inheritance has been a bugbear of mine for some time, well, I'm afraid I — '

'Went on and on about it,' Henry commented dryly.

'So much so that I might not have been as attentive of my children as I should've been. Portia has overheard us arguing a few times. Then when you arrived, and she saw your likeness to her great-grandmother, she put two and two together. With a child's logic she thought you'd come to take everything away from us.' Priscilla smoothed down her daughter's messy hair. 'Go on, darling.'

Portia started crying in earnest. 'I'm so sorry. I didn't mean for you to get hurt! I just wanted to scare you away so Mummy could be happy. So I put a big spider in your room and loosened Coco's saddle. I'm really sorry!'

'Ah, the saddle,' said Justine. That hadn't been an accident, as she'd begun to suspect.

'But it was wrong,' said Priscilla, her eyes welling up too in response to her daughter's tears. '*I* was in the wrong. I knew the situation when I married

Henry and should've let it be. And I shouldn't have argued with him in front of the children. Because of it you could've been seriously hurt when you fell off the horse.'

She hugged Cordelia close as she sat on Justine's bed. 'Then you saved Dilly. She might have died if it hadn't been for you, and I want to thank you. From the bottom of my heart. Richard told us how your parents kept you for themselves when everyone presumed you were dead. What they did was wrong, very wrong, but I remember my own feelings when Portia was born; I loved her the moment I held her in my arms, so I understand why they did it. And I'm really sorry that I wasn't very nice to you. I hope you can forgive me. I realise now that I don't actually care about inheriting Stonybrook. As long as I have my family.'

Henry took his wife's hand. 'To be honest, it's a bit of a shock to know that I have a cousin, but it kind of explains it all. I used to think that I was somehow falling short of Grandfather's expectations, and that's why he changed his will, but I can see now it was because he knew you were still alive. And I approve of my circus cousin. Very much so.'

He shrugged, a little embarrassed, and everyone laughed, even Portia who dried her eyes and smeared more grime over her face. The tension in the room lifted, and Justine reached for Portia's hand.

'What you did to the saddle was very dangerous, but I think you already know that. Fortunately I've learned how to fall safely. And both of you climbing on up that branch, that was very dangerous too.'

Portia nodded.

'But I'm impressed that you both managed to swing yourselves up there.' Justine winked at her. 'Tom cut off the lower branches.'

Portia blushed but didn't pull away. 'I borrowed Tom's ladder.'

'Yes, we must do something about

that,' said Tom dryly. 'Seems we can't trust you around keys and ladders.'

Portia turned to him, wide-eyed. 'I'll never do anything like that again!'

Tom sent her a long look. 'No, I don't believe you will.'

'Never ever,' said Dilly for emphasis.

'But still,' said her father, frowning, 'what *were* you thinking? And why didn't you stop your sister, Portia, if you felt it wasn't safe?'

Tears welled up in Portia's eyes again. 'I didn't know it was going to break. I told her not to climb to the end but she wouldn't listen. I'm so sorry!'

Sighing, Henry put his arm around her. 'Well, I guess we're all relieved that no one has come to serious harm, but Mum and I are going to have a long talk about what to do with the pair of you. Mischief is one thing, but causing other people hurt and putting yourselves in danger is quite another.'

Portia sniffed. 'Oh Daddy! I miss you and Mummy, and I don't have any friends at school.'

'Yeah, they all hate her,' Cordelia added helpfully.

Priscilla slid her arm around Henry's waist. 'Perhaps a local school? And we could move to the home farm as you suggested. Do it up and run holiday lets. It'd be a new beginning. For all of us,' she added and looked at Justine with friendly eyes, for the first time.

A new beginning, thought Justine. Everyone's lives had certainly taken a turn in the direction of the unknown, her own probably more than anyone else's. It was a lot to take in, but there was one change that did not have to happen.

'No,' she said. 'I don't want you to lose your home. You're the lady of the manor, Priscilla, and you're good at it and all that it entails. That's not what I want to be.'

Her grandfather who had remained quiet throughout the tearful revelations cleared his throat. 'Your generosity does you credit, my dear. And yours too, Priscilla.'

Priscilla sent him a bewildered look.

'Yes, I realise I may have been mistaken in you,' Richard continued. 'I thought you married my grandson for his expectations, and because of what I regarded as irritating presumptions on your part, I made it known that I'd changed my will. But I hadn't. I always intended the baronetcy to stay with the manor, and therefore with Henry, and for Justine to have the home farm. It's the only thing that makes sense.'

Henry pulled his wife close. 'I know that's what you thought, Grandfather,' he admonished mildly, 'but I've never doubted Priscilla's love for me. There's a lot more to a marriage than what others may see.'

Richard nodded. 'Indeed there is. And I'm happy to admit I was wrong. I know you feel Stonybrook to be a burden — '

'No, Grandfather,' Henry interrupted. 'I have always loved Stonybrook. It's the only home I've known, it's my family's home, and I've hated the thought that one day we'd have to leave it and so to lessen the pain persuaded myself that I'd like a different kind of life. But I would be honoured to one day hold the title of Lord Brooks and run Stonybrook.' He held his hand out to his grandfather with tears in his eyes.

Richard clasped Henry's hand and took a few moments to compose himself. 'So, to business. I'm not dead yet,' he said with a smile, 'and still have a few plans for the estate. I want the menagerie re-opened, with Tom and Justine in charge. Holiday lets, Priscilla, are an excellent idea.'

Priscilla beamed.

'Perhaps we should consider opening parts of the house to the public,' he continued. 'We have a few treasures here that are worth sharing with the world. Maybe even let a circus overwinter on our land from time to time.'

Portia and Cordelia squealed with delight at that, but a raised finger and a stern look from Henry reminded them that the potential presence of a circus was not an invitation to further mischief.

'To survive in the modern world,' said Richard, 'Stonybrook and the home farm have to be enterprises, and we must think creatively. All suggestions welcome.'

The family — *her* family — clustered excitedly around Justine's bed for a little while longer discussing plans and ideas for the estate until her grandfather, on catching her eye, pleaded tiredness and requested in an imperious manner for Henry and his family to take him home.

Which left only Tom.

'Please tell me . . . '

'I didn't . . . '

They spoke simultaneously, and Tom grinned.

'You first,' he said.

'I'd rather you went first.'

'Okay, then. I was going to say that I didn't know your history. The likeness between you and your grandmother is striking but it honestly never clicked for me. I can see you must've thought so, maybe that I wanted you because of it. That isn't the case. You must believe me.'

'I do,' she replied.

Tom's eyebrows rose in surprise, and the tension left his face. 'You do?'

'Your reaction to me confirmed it when I asked you what you really knew about me. But for what it's worth, I never thought you could be that two-faced.'

Visibly relieved, his shoulders dropped, and he took her good hand. 'Thank you for having faith in me. Was that what you wanted to say?'

'Yes. I couldn't bear the thought that you might've been playing me. Like Richard and my parents did.'

'But only because they had your best interests at heart, and wanted to keep you safe.' At her surprise he added, 'Richard told me. When you were in surgery. The whole sorry tale about George. How you're lucky to be alive. And after today as well.'

Justine swallowed hard. 'Does Henry know?' He'd have been about eleven when his father died but even so, to be told your father was a murderer . . .

'No. One day Richard will tell him, but for now there's been enough upheaval.'

That's how Justine would have handled it, had she been in her grandfather's shoes, but it still felt awful to conceal a secret from the one person it truly concerned. She hoped the old man didn't leave it too long.

'So . . . ' she said.

'So,' he said, 'what about us? Is there still an 'us'? I know you've been through a lot lately and that you wanted to leave but . . . ' He shrugged awkwardly.

She squeezed his hand. 'Of course there is. Life is going to be pretty tough for me for the foreseeable future. I'll need you with me. A right hand man, if you like,' she added in the hope of lightening the mood. There was still an issue they hadn't touched upon.

Tom remained serious. 'When the

ambulance crew brought you here, and you'd lost so much blood, I thought you were going to die. This may sound strange but it was as if my whole life had been preparing me for meeting you, despite all the things I've done and people I've known, even all the decisions I've made, good as well as bad. It was meant to happen, I just didn't realise it. And when you lay there so pale . . . '

He cleared his throat, and Justine reached out and tousled his mane of auburn hair. It needed brushing and tidying up but felt incredibly soft too. Just like Tom himself. Soft and gentle underneath all that manly ruggedness. But still very much a man, and perfect for her.

'I'm all right,' she said. 'Think I'm made of sterner stuff than that.'

'I think you're like Rexus. Strong, beautiful, majestic.'

She laughed. 'But can I be tamed, you're thinking?'

'I don't want to tame you. I want you to be who you are.' Tom smiled back at her, then his smile morphed into a cheeky grin. 'You say you're all right? Does that mean you're well enough for me to kiss you?'

'I'm a little sore, but I'm not going to break. So yes, I think I can handle that.'

Without another word Tom pulled her close, and she buried her good hand in his hair and gave herself up to his lingering kiss. She didn't want to tame him either.

Except maybe his hair. Just a little.

Other titles in the
Linford Romance Library:

LOVE AND LIES

Jenny Worstall

When Rosie Peach arrives for her interview to become Shaston Convent School's new piano teacher, the first person she meets is striking music master David Hart. As her new role gets underway, Rosie comes up against several obstacles: her predecessor Miss Spiker's infamous temper, a bunch of unruly but loveable schoolgirls, and her swiftly growing feelings for David. The nuns of the convent are determined to meddle their way towards a school romance, but David is a complex character, and Rosie can't help but wonder what secrets he is hiding . . .

GAY DEFEAT

Denise Robins

Disarmingly lovely, Delia Beringham is the only daughter of a wealthy financier who indulges her every whim. It is Delia's hope that her lover, Lionel Hewes, will leave his wife for her — but the sudden crash of the Beringham family fortune and her father's suicide change all that. Lionel abruptly fades from the picture, and Delia is left with only her own courage and determination to sustain her. So what is she to say when her father's friend, Martin Revell, chivalrously offers her his hand in marriage?

LORD SAWSBURY SEEKS A BRIDE

Fenella J. Miller

If he is to protect his estate and save his sister from penury, Lord Simon Sawsbury must marry an heiress. Annabel Burgoyne has no desire to marry, but wishes to please her parents, who are offering a magnificent dowry in the hope of enticing an impecunious aristocrat. As Simon and Bella, along with their families, move to their Grosvenor Square residences for the Season, it's not long before the neighbours are drawn together. But when events go from bad to worse, will Simon sacrifice his reputation to marry Bella?

MURDER AT THE HIGHLAND PRACTICE

Jo Bartlett

Shortly after her return to the Scottish Highlands, DI Blair Hannah's small team of detectives is called upon to investigate a suspicious death in the rural town of Balloch Pass. The elderly woman had altered her will before she died, leaving everything to two unlikely beneficiaries: the local priest, and the town's new GP, Dr Noah Bradshaw. As Blair races against time to catch a potential killer, can she beat the ghosts of her past and grab the chance of her own happy ever after?

MACGREGOR'S COVE

June Davies

Running the Bell Inn, which sits high above Macgregor's Cove, is a busy yet peaceful life for Amaryllis's family — but their lodger Kit Chesterton arrives with a heavy secret in tow, which threatens to disturb the quiet waters. Meanwhile, a recent influx in contraband starts ripples of suspicion about smugglers, and Amaryllis's sister sets her sights on Adam Whitlock, who has recently returned from India with a shady companion. Despite the sinister events washing through the Cove, love surfaces as friendship becomes romance and strangers become family.

LEGAL EAGLES

Rebecca Holmes

Newly qualified solicitor Helen Martin has just moved to a new area to start a job in an old-fashioned family firm, hoping to escape the problems of her past. Here she meets Peter, who has a story of his own; but they soon discover that the past has a habit of throwing obstacles in the way. And while the senior partner of Helen's firm struggles when his estranged son reappears, it seems that the love-birds' paths might already be more intertwined than they could have imagined . . .